ENCHANTED
SUMMER

ENCHANTED SUMMER

Gabrielle Roy

translated from the French by
Joyce Marshall

McCLELLAND AND STEWART

To Berthe,

to my neighbours at Grande-Pointe in Charlevoix County

and to the children of all seasons with the wish that they will never tire of listening to their planet Earth.

BOOKS BY GABRIELLE ROY

The Cashier
Enchanted Summer
The Hidden Mountain
The Road Past Altamont
Street of Riches
The Tin Flute
Where Nests the Water Hen
Windflower

CONTENTS

Monsieur Toong

I

The bullfrog lived on the edge of the inhabited world. You went to the end of the village, which is already somewhat remote, and now there was just enough room between the wooded mountain and the wild shore for the railway line. Only its single track could manage to insinuate itself between the rubble of rock on one side and the piled-up boulders on the other.

Nowhere else in the world have I encountered such a tranquil railroad.

Right beside it lies the river, which has all the room it needs to extend its great tide-racked body for a breadth of twenty-two miles. At flood tide, waves splash against the embankment; at times you can hear the sound high on the rocky hillside as if the waves were breaking within the stone. On the crest are some ancient, rarely silent pines. One, flung out on the slant, mourns with a curious insistence just before the fading of the light.

Another surprise too; all along the track wildflowers grow in profusion as if, once accustomed to the exhalations of the engines and the poverty of the soil, they find certain rare advantages here. They are never browsed and, furthermore, seldom picked. There is no one to speak of but Berthe and me to pick them. And we are always reasonable, Berthe and I. We are careful not to pull them up by the roots and we never take more than enough for a bunch apiece.

At the end of fifteen or twenty minutes' walk far from all habitation, after a sharp bend where everything threatens to tip into the river, you come to a very desolate spot. In the shadow of a rock-face rising sheer as a chimney lies a pool of perfectly black water. At daybreak it may be gay and sparkling but this cannot last for long since the space is restricted, the mountain high, and the sun has soon circled the cape. This rock chimney is undoubtedly compelled to live the greater part of its life in shadow—even more so the pool at its foot. Yet it was here that the bullfrog lived, in this cold sad water. However, as you will see very soon by the way we made his acquaintance, it was not out of misanthropy that he lived so far from others.

Perhaps like the flowers on the track—the evening primroses, the columbines and the bluebells—or even the tall isolated pine on the cliff, he had weighed the pros and cons of solitude and discovered that it offered more benefits than drawbacks.

Berthe and I were coming along the railway track one evening, talking cheerfully, for we always feel gay and light-hearted when we are leaving people and houses behind to rejoin nature, just as we are always happy on the way back, to be returning to people and houses.

Doubtless, in the semi-obscurity of the twilight, that moment of complete attention when nothing could be heard but the sounds of the water and the pine, the unwonted explosion of human voices in laughing and noisy exchange must have aroused the bullfrog's curiosity. And clearly this curiosity became unabashed interest for we had just reached the sharp bend near the pool when out sprang a most cordial greeting, "Toong!"

You would have thought that somewhere under the water a playful musician had plucked a submerged guitar.

In this deserted spot amid the swiftly advancing evening shadows, the friendly salutation was so unexpected we were left speechless for a moment. Standing two steps from the inky water, so lifeless and without a wrinkle on its surface, I finally replied quite at random, "Toong!"

The reply was immediate, "Toong! Toong!"

Berthe and I exchanged glances. Were we dealing with a prankster? Or with some poor hermit so delighted to have someone to talk to that he scarcely knew what he was saying? We determined to find out.

"Toong! Toong! Toong!" said Berthe.

At once the reply emerged from the pool, "Toong! Toong! Toong! Toong!"

The syllables were quite detached; there was no question about it, we were being answered each time by an additional toong. Was this how bullfrogs conversed? Or might this one be a bit simple-minded? It was all rather puzzling. I tried again.

"Toong! Toong! Toong! Toong!"

From the pool came curtly, "Toong! Toong!"

The tone was a shade impatient also as if, without losing his good humour, the bullfrog was trying to point out, "You must be brief. Your long human sentences drag out so."

This gave us something to think about. Without insisting further, we left our conversation with the bullfrog there and hurried on to the trout stream, which we like to visit once each summer. Under a screen of broad damp foliage, it gurgles loudly, like a bottle being emptied.

In the gathering dusk we didn't linger. Just long enough to make sure the bottle was still being joyfully emptied. And then we retraced our steps.

It was almost night when we passed by the pool

again. No sound indicated life. The birds had suspended all movement. Even the quivering pines scarcely murmured now, as if to trouble us as little as possible with the tale of their persistent loneliness. It was hard to believe in our lively conversation only an hour before with the invisible occupant of the pool.

Disappointed, I called loudly, "Monsieur Toong!"

The place, so solitary, seemed astonished by the noise and did not deign to answer by as much as the faintest ruffling of leaves.

"Monsieur Toong!" Berthe called in her turn.

Nothing.

"Monsieur Toong, are you asleep?" I asked. "You're asleep now, Monsieur Toong?"

Then from the depths of a profound slumber, as if from the bottom of the sea, a faint sound emerged—sluggish and drawn out, friendly still but with undertones of "Just when I was sleeping so soundly"—"To-o-ong!"

We hadn't the heart to persist but stole away on tiptoe.

"With frogs," said Berthe, "who knows, it may be as it is with people, the first sleep is crucial. Sometimes when I'm wakened out of my first sleep, I can't drop off again."

We felt rather regretful at having perhaps disturbed the bullfrog's repose.

"I daresay he begins his day very early, with the sun," I said. "It must touch his pool first."

"In any case," said Berthe, "playing the guitar under water, and in perpetual dimness, must be exhausting. At night Monsieur Toong must be dead tired."

II

One calm cool evening the following summer, we were hurrying to reach Monsieur Toong's hideaway before nightfall. The hour of our walk coincided, as we had intended, with that of the high tide. The river sings then, full to the brim. Its song quickens our pace. Yet on the railway track our steps cannot help but be unequal from tie to tie—one short, two long, two short, one long, rather like Morse code adapted for feet. Walking quickly becomes tiring but no matter; a difficulty we impose upon ourselves for enjoyment is a pleasure in the end.

The waves broke with a quiet sound, very gently and without haste, on the boulders the railway workers pile along the roadbed each year to keep it from sliding into the water. Even so, it is slipping in by degrees and will finally be engulfed completely, I suppose, for it is only by constant petitions that our little railway line is kept alive.

Far away on the rippled water of the channel an ancient black freighter drifted without leaving any wake, just as solitary as the railway and seemingly as lacking in destination.

From some distance away we heard the grieving pine. High on the rock it complained gently. Yet there was almost no moving air that evening. Where then had the pine found enough to make its grieving song? Perhaps in the dense woods behind the rocks, from which it had detached itself one day to come and live alone on this sentinel post.

Everywhere, like acquaintances, we found the little flowers of the previous summer: the evening primroses, whose delicate faces open only towards the closing of the day; bluebells drawing from the grudging soil their blooms of clearest azure; the tall Easter candles of mullein; vetch too, that ancient companion of almost deserted railway tracks; and wild roses. Apparently everything that does not die from the harshness of its life acquires more sturdiness and health than it would in gentler places.

Even before we had reached that sharp bend where telephone pole, rails and rock threatened to capsize, impatient to renew relations with the bullfrog, I called, "Hi there, Monsieur Toong! Are you still of this world?"

I hadn't even finished when the answer rang out, joyful and clear, "Toong!"

I can't deny that my heart turned over.

"Is it really you?"

"Toong! Toong!"

"And me? Do you recognize me?"

"Toong! Toong! Toong! As if there could be more than two people who'd come and talk to an old hermit in the lonesome twilight."

"And me?" Berthe asked.

"Toong! Toong! Toong! Toong!" Monsieur Toong assured her affably.

It was the same as last year. Our friend never went beyond four toongs; he then invariably returned to two. It was all a bit baffling and the bullfrog seemed to enjoy his little game.

One thing was new, though; this time Monsieur Toong came to the edge of the pool to talk to us. He climbed as high as he could without slipping on the wet bank and here found a purchase for his two front feet. From beneath a very shallow film of water he studied us with a sort of anxious friendliness. He was of good size and of jovial mien, making at least four of an ordinary frog. He spoke to us in music from close at hand and so we were able to see just how a bullfrog plays the guitar.

He swelled, swelled, swelled his throat, the flabby skin stretching like a leather bottle filling with water. His huge eyes bulged with the effort. The pockets of his cheeks seemed ready to burst. Now we had seen how much effort it cost the musician to produce a single note. Finally he released all the air that had puffed him up like a balloon and we heard the incomparable sound, "Toong!"

"Bravo!" we congratulated but did not ask any more of him.

14

We understood at last why you must not try to engage in lengthy conversations with a creature like Monsieur Toong, for whom every sound is exhausting.

With regret just the same we said, "Good night, Monsieur Toong. Keep well ... till next time ... Monsieur Toong," all the while hurrying off to outstrip the night, which advances very quickly in the almost perpetual shadow of these rocks.

A few pleasant, drawn-out toongs accompanied us— a little sad too perhaps as if from the dark water we were being reminded, "Come back. Don't let too much time go by. Life is short."

III

Once again we returned on an evening of calm weather to the black secret pool at the base of the sheer chimney of rock. This time too we had both the high tide and coolness to chase away insects and, I suppose, the mood to appreciate such things.

The water splashed against the embankment, the solitary pine transformed into a mild complaint a bit of air that came to it from far away, bluebells chimed without sound. But our pool, when we reached it in the last glimmers of the twilight, was silent. Terribly silent. Suddenly it made one think of the shadowy depthless water under the trapdoor of an oubliette.

On its banks we called in turn, "Monsieur Toong? Have you gone? Or are you just playing dead?"

Nothing replied but the song sparrow, who suddenly broke off his roundelay as if it had occurred to him, at hearings news asked of Monsieur Toong, "That's true, what indeed has become of Monsieur Toong? We haven't heard of him around here, if I'm not mistaken, for many months."

But too heartless to concern himself for long with the fate of the bullfrog, he hopped from one branch to another, shaking the elder-bush in which he was hidden, and without further ado resumed his endless refrain.

From whom else could we ask news?

I picked up a stone and flung it into the middle of the pool. Water gushed upwards. Circles spread, widening, over the surface. At the same moment a shape appeared among the rushes at the base of the mountain, a long-legged bird that at once withdrew a little farther into its hiding place.

Berthe's quick eye had recognized a little heron.

"Maybe it was the heron," she said thoughtfully, "that did away with Monsieur Toong."

"Quite so, quite so," an aged crow, a familiar of these parts, informed us in passing.

Then she circled the cape, and the silence that enclosed us was like the silence that falls when the story has been told, the outcome divulged and the words "the end" inserted at the foot of a page.

We returned haltingly, our steps now lengthened to reach a more widely spaced tie, now shortened so as not to trip over its neighbour. We had no more inclination for talk. The old pine, high on the rock, still hummed softly in snatches, between silences when it seemed to be drifting off to sleep. Water splashed as merrily as ever against the boulders of the embankment. From far away, at certain turnings, borne on a brisk current of air, came a few last echoes of the joyous drunkard under the broad leaves, drinking right out of the bottle.

But to us now it was rather as if this corner of the world had been emptied.

Monsieur Emile's Gatte

The word must have been invented by Monsieur Emile, one of many he invented in the course of his life. He was a man with a bent for creating expressions to his own taste for objects that seemed to him poorly named or whose dictionary appellation he didn't know. He was equally ingenious at eking out a living from a parsimonious soil, for this was still the time when one could manage to subsist from the fruit of a multiplicity of small activities: maple sugar in the spring, a bit of hay in summer, eel fishing in the fall, and in winter chopping wood.

Monsieur Emile's farm stood off to one side, against the base of the mountain. It was composed of a number of little fields of various shapes scattered here and there around the road and sundry natural objects: a diamond below the dirt road; a square near the house; farther along, beside the brook, a sort of deeply curved arc; even a circle around a huge stone no one had ever been able to move. Of all this Monsieur Emile made good use; from the square he obtained potatoes, from the bent arc fine

17

clover, from the circle around the stone millet in abundance. And from all sorts of other bits and pieces hay that he cut with a scythe.

Towards the end of the summer there was no trimmer sight than Monsieur Emile's farm as, pipe in mouth, his great scythe in his hand and a whetstone in the pocket of his trousers, he tidied up the borders of his innumerable enclosures. Soon not a blade of grass escaped from fields that were now as smooth as the ancient rock in their midst. Only his gatte defeated him.

A patch of spongy ground, uneven, always damp, it was pitiable beside the other well-kept fields. It couldn't be drained. Nothing grew in it but a sort of coarse couch grass. Nevertheless, in the interests of neatness, Monsieur Emile fenced in his gatte. He did it in the old-fashioned way with roughly split rails set one upon the other snaking around the wretched bit of ground. Thus tidily set apart, the poor gatte looked at least a little less abandoned. But for a long time still it was to remain unproductive, a disgrace to Monsieur Emile, who could not hide it from view, exposed as it was right beside the road for all to see.

Came the day when, unable to put a refractory cow with the others, Monsieur Emile had the idea of confining her for a few days' penitence in the gatte, never suspecting that the action would be rich in consequence. For in no time the cow, Rouquette by name, had uprooted the couch grass that was stifling all other vegetation. Then, bored in her solitude, she took to turning and turning on the spot, a hundred times, a thousand. She dug the hollows in the soil even deeper with her hooves and everywhere she spread her dung.

Thus all was made ready for the miracle of next spring.

For in the desolate gatte, pitted all over like an old sieve, there appeared a plant unknown in these parts till now. On each of the driest hummocks in the muddy ground it bloomed in great clusters of that marvellous rosy pink of certain sunsets in the country. You might have thought it the modest ancestor of the glorious oleander. It was kalmia, discovered by the Swedish botanist, Peter Kalm, and dedicated to him by his master, Linnaeus. Covered in old rose, the gatte looked young and gay.

But where had the graceful flower come from? Far away in its dense colonies in Baie-des-Rochers had it heard that Monsieur Emile's gatte was more hospitable to its species now that Rouquette had turned and turned about and enriched the soil? Was it carried there on the wind? Or by the birds? Or perhaps the seed had been present already, so deeply embedded in the ground there was no chance of its climbing to the light on its own. And Rouquette, frenzied with boredom, by trampling the soil, finally brought it to the surface. I for one incline to this version and I also believe that, having exhumed the seed, she then nourished it with her dung.

The kalmia blossom only lasts for a month or so. But the shrub had gained a firm foothold in the ancient gatte. And next spring the rosy clusters on each dry hummock were twice as thick as the previous year. The folk of the region now knew where to find the pretty flowers that to some recalled the azalea and to others the oleander. As you passed along the dirt road you could see in many windows, amid geraniums and fuchsias, bunches of kalmia in old mustard or peanut butter jars.

But plants are like people. The moment a group is happily settled somewhere, everyone wants to move in. Scarcely was the kalmia installed than all around it were blue flags. The two did not harm one another though, for while the kalmia sought out the driest spots, the flags delighed in the oozy hollows. Buttercups crowded in between them. The old gatte, all rosy pink the year before,

19

was this year of varied colours. In autumn goldenrod and long-leafed asters circled the stagnant water that glimmered faintly in all the little hollows of the gatte. And these minuscule holes, each scarcely bigger than an eye, managed to reflect the long gilded plumage of the goldenrod, the delicate muted lilac of the asters, a bit of sky, passing clouds and even, on occasion, the flight of some bird of land or sea.

So because Monsieur Emile, a careful man, enclosed this bit of a field and put a balky cow to graze there one day, the untilled soil was in a fair way to becoming the most inviting spot in the region. Right until freeze-up there were flowers, colours, and a sort of life that seemed more tender and more gentle than elsewhere.

But you will say, in the winter, covered with snow in the bitter cold, especially at the desolate hour of nightfall, the gatte must look precisely what it is—an old, saturated sponge.

Well, no. Quite the reverse. For, you remember, the gatte is at the edge of our settlement, right at the foot of the mountain. So that before it circles behind the cape, the sun always stops momentarily on this field. For that instant it is completely illuminated, as if by a strange searchlight; the pallid lifeless snow becomes at the centre pink like the kalmia, along the edges blue like the flags, and here and there it lights up with the glowing hue of the dead goldenrod. For three or four minutes each day the gatte is radiant with the most marvellous colours of the summer. Then it sinks into the night.

Aimé's Cows

I always cut across the fields when I go to my neighbour's. Aimé's cows, at my passage, stop grazing. They
raise their heads and look at me, following me with their
eyes as if to place me once for all. I don't know why cows
are called stupid. The expression of these three, as they
examine me closely and note details, clearly shows a sort
of reflection.

"Ah good. It's the lady from the summer cottage, on
her way again to our master's. The one who comes from
the city. Who spends the summers here."

And back they go to their quiet grazing. Proof that
their minds must work in much this way is that if I go by
again ten minutes later, they consider me briefly without
bothering to stop grazing or raise their heads, as if they
were concluding, "The same as before."

But if I don't pass by for two or three hours, the
whole performance begins over; they follow me with
their eyes with renewed curiosity. And then finally,
"Why, yes. It's the lady of this morning. The one from
the cottage. The one who comes from the city. The one

who goes to our master's a hundred times a day."

It's as if they lacked memory rather than sense.

Or as if they were as absent-minded as certain people who "can't quite place" their acquaintances.

My theory no longer holds. Today I walked twice through the pasture at intervals of an hour. The second time like the first the cows stopped grazing. Examined me at length. Stared at me, you might say. Showed the same curiosity as two hours earlier. As the day before.

I spoke of it to Aimé.

"Do they recognize me, do you think? Are they able to recognize people?"

"Ah yes."

"Then?"

. . .

"So? They find me so astonishing?"

Aimé politely, "That may be . . . at times."

Jeannot the Crow

I

Nothing in this world is more difficult than to distinguish one crow from another. If I was finally able to recognize Jeannot, this was because he came without fail on days when the wind sang from the southwest, to perch in the delicate tip of my wild red cherry tree and let himself be rocked for a long time, the tree in this summer wind being simply a swing in the sky.

None of our other trees can be compared to this wild red cherry. We began to shape it when it was still a sapling, pruning here, straightening there, rectifying this; and just as with human beings when you apply yourself to them in time and gently, we obtained astonishing results. The tree is so striking now that it is always compared to something other than a tree. In repose, with the wind playing on it with muted strings, it is a lyre. Viewed from below and a slight distance, it looks like a vase overflowing with flowers on a shelf above the ocean. When the wild wind flings its leaves forward as if over a face, it suggests a young woman shaking and shaking her outspread hair with joyful movements of the head. However, it is in the southwest wind with Jeannot at its tip that our wild red cherry tree is most graceful.

Many of our friends exclaim when they visit us for the first time, "What a beautiful tree! Where did it come from? From what country?"

At first we used to reply that it was an ordinary little tree of a sort that grows all along the cliff, native to these parts, nothing more. That we'd only had to prune it a trifle, encourage it, give it water and fertilizer. Now we feel compassion for the bewilderment these simple remarks always awaken on people's faces, as if they can't bear the idea that they might do as much. Perhaps it's having to do as much that appals them. Now when our guests exclaim, "What a tree! You must have had it brought from far away," we say nothing to make them think otherwise. And in one sense it's true that our wild red cherry tree comes from far away.

As you might expect, the birds are very much attached to it. With most of them, it must be admitted, from self-interest. A few years ago I noticed that cedar waxwings, beguiling birds with crew cuts, arrived almost every day in July, seven or eight of them together, to perch here and there in the tree. After a while I realized that they had come to see whether the little fruit, which were just beginning to take colour, would soon be good to eat. At last one day they were ready and in an instant the tree was stripped. For the rest of that summer I never saw another cedar waxwing.

But the following summer they were outwitted. Six big blue jays in company discovered that there were some of these exquisite fruit in our yard. Through the red clusters one morning I glimpsed their brilliant uniforms of cobalt blue. The shriek of a soul in agony rose a short distance away where a seventh jay stood sentinel, and nothing is less appropriate to these splendid uhlans than this truly terrible shriek. Seated in the tree, the six jays feasted. The berries, however, weren't quite ripe. The cedar waxwings had dropped by the previous day to taste them and had decided to give them one more day. Much good it did them. When they returned on the morrow, the cupboard was bare.

But the next summer the blue jays were forestalled in turn. Evening grosbeaks, seemingly less finicky than the greedy jays, arrived early one July morning and cleaned the cherry tree of its small fruit while they were still green. Perhaps it gave them indigestion. Served them right.

But let me come at last to my subject, for if I've mentioned these successive raids, it was to show the difference between Jeannot and other birds. He at least came to the tree neither to eat nor even to sleep but only, as far as I could tell, from affection.

I daresay he pilfered elsewhere. A bit to the right, a bit to the left, so that it was not too apparent in any one garden: for instance, a leaf of red lettuce from Lucienne, my third neighbour—and how could a crow fail to appreciate the tasty lettuce that we were all constantly begging for ourselves?; perhaps a few sweet juicy cherries from Berthe; and here and there, from people who still had the heart to grow them, that delicacy of all crows, the seeds of those giant sunflowers that used to bloom everywhere of old. But from me Jeannot took nothing.

Besides, he came only when the rocking wind blew, bowing our little tree endlessly against the background of sea. Days without wind and without music, "dead" days when I myself grow lonely—perhaps for eternity—there was no sign of Jeannot. But as soon as the song of the rustling leaves resumed, I could be sure I'd see my crow again. Shortly afterwards, in fact, I would discern in the intensely blue sky an approaching speck of black.

Sometimes he'd have trouble navigating so as to land precisely in the middle of the cherry tree. He'd be obliged to repeat his approach again and again, carried each time into the distance. He'd then glide on motionless wings, and to recover his speed and momentum, he'd turn at the base of the mountain where the air is always calm. At last he would manage to make a perfect landing on his little perch. This was a tiny fork formed by two supple twigs high in the tree. Once settled and sure of his equilibrium, Jeannot would relax and let himself be carried fearlessly from one side of the horizon to the other.

In this way, by certain infallible signs, I learned a few years ago to recognize a friendly crow.

Jeannot never slept in the tree. With the field glasses I would see his eyes glinting in his black shiny face. Nor did he give any of those caws that grate so on the nerves. He was quite silent. He seemed to be there only to dream while contemplating the mountains, the whitecaps on the river and, far in the distance, the line of the south shore, always somewhat hazy on warm days. Like a small black lookout in the crow's-nest of a ship, he swung back and forth in the sky.

By other characteristics too—a way of holding his head to one side, a stiffness in his right wing as if it had once been slightly injured—I became better and better able to recognize my gentle crow. I could finally follow most of the activities and movements of his life.

First of all, where he spent the night. In a tree but this as different from our little wild red cherry as day is from night. A tall melancholy tree, shaggy, dead on one side and with numerous long branches, some dry, others leafy, a very old maple with room, storey upon storey, for the whole tribe to settle at nightfall, in families. At the end of a wild field, on a desolate plateau in a remote spot and with sombre woods in the background, it had been known for as long as anyone remembered as the Tree of

Crows. When they gathered there at dusk, the tree, already dark by nature, looked truly fearsome with those little pitch-black shapes pressed against one another along all the branches, even the skeletal ones. What did it look like then? Well, what else but a scarecrow made of crows?

To those of the species who didn't lack humour or a comic sense, it was perhaps amusing to inhabit a tree that seemed designed to scare them away.

At sunrise, however, nothing was gayer for a brief moment than that ancient tree with all its tenants in a great commotion of departure, giving voice to resounding caws. The new light awoke iridescences in the lustrous plumage that the vainest among them were still polishing with their beaks. Then they rose together into the sky and the old maple fell back into its mournful solitude.

The crows then broke ranks. Some, the more sociable, proceeded to the charming town of Baie-Saint-Paul where there were well-tended gardens to pillage. Others chose the uninhabited wild region of the abandoned pool of Monsieur Toong, the bullfrog. Still others remained in Petite-Rivière-Saint-François and spent their days flying round the mountain and along the shore of the river.

My Jeannot was rather solitary; by day he seldom rejoined his kin. He was even less inclined to fraternize with the gulls gathered in compact groups on the rocks uncovered by the receding tide. A few crows risked it, however, and there was no more curious sight in the empty immensity of the river than this close companionship on the crests of breakers of black birds and white birds. When I examined them with field glasses, however, I never caught them conversing with one another. They were together, it's true, but apparently without any sort of communication. And from afar, thus assembled and yet not acquainted, they resembled human beings.

What did Jeannot do all day? Unquestionably, if the wind was favourable, not much else but rock in the tree. He also pilfered a bit from the gardens to right and left. As his territory was so restricted, he finally drew attention to himself and in the course of the summer I began to hear threatening remarks directed at Jeannot.

"That dratted crow!" grumbled Monsieur Simon, my neighbour. "I'll settle his hash!"

As excuse for Monsieur Simon and several other enemies of the crows, I should mention the trouble they'd had that year rescuing their fruit and vegetables from caterpillars, slugs and potato bugs. And now it looked as if the crows would snatch what remained from under their noses. Yet it seemed unjust to me that all the blame should fall on the head of poor Jeannot, who was perhaps less prompt than other crows to make off when Monsieur Simon approached, sweeping the air with his arms and shouting, "Dratted crow! Dratted crow!"

Besides, how could Monsieur Simon imagine that he was always dealing with the same crow, since he had never learned to distinguish one from another with the eyes of affection?

However, while believing that he was speaking each day to the same crow, Monsieur Simon managed to offend a good many birds—from the most scatterbrained to the oldest and most dignified. The tribe finally banded together to harass this man of such little perspicacity. From then on there was always one looting his garden while another drew his attention elsewhere.

He took to lying in ambush in his lilac hedge, loaded rifle in hand. One afternoon I thought I heard through the rustling of the leaves the sound of a shot from the garden next door. I was very anxious for a few minutes.

But soon, a black speck in the radiant immensity, Jeannot appeared. He came, moreover, from the opposite direction to the dangerous garden. For that day at least he had not joined in the foray against Monsieur Simon.

He sank to his perch as gently as a flower drops from its stem. He remained for a good twenty minutes that day, I believe, huddled in his little niche, journeying across the sky.

II

The next month was one of the most pleasant I can remember. The southwest wind filled the air almost continually with the roaring of a river that must have flowed for days and days. All living creatures were lulled by this strange and mysterious river, Jeannot in the cherry tree, I in my wooden swing, Aimé's cows motionless at my fence, delivered for one more day from gnats and horseflies. From moment to moment, borne on the moving air as if on a high and sonorous wave, sounded the melodious tinkle of the bell the Rover set in motion each time she craned her neck to reach over the hedge for a cool leaf.

This blessed wind I imagine as having been born in a distant happy country where beings never hunt one another but live quietly side by side. Furthermore, I noticed that it was only on such days that the black birds on the exposed rocks far away in the murmuring water joined with the white birds.

My Jeannot arrived almost every day now at a regular hour. He came to rest between two thefts. Mere trifles: a leaf of Lucienne's fine lettuce, a strawberry at Berthe's and, more serious, three pecks from a tomato that might never heal.

"That cursed black devil!" I thought I heard in the distance.

Completely safe with me, wings pressed to his body and head tucked in, Jeannot travelled through the sky.

There were calm periods. Then the wind stilled and, the music of the foliage abruptly silent, we were back feet first in what is called "reality," and it seemed insufficient, confining, intolerable. But soon the atmosphere would resound again with the stereophonic music of those summer days in the country.

Truly it is a complex music and requires the participation of many players. To my left, the house of my closest neighbour is enclosed by a group of old willow trees with heavy branches. It is here the wind attacks. As it forces a passage through the low and often deformed branches, it acquires that deep voice of a powerful river. You can hear the abundant water, at once free and confined, discharging no one knows where. This is the bass that supports the voices of the more subtle instruments. Suddenly the wind has crossed the road and given the signal to my pines. Nothing is silkier than their masses of fine needles and here the wind stirs eddy after eddy. In these eddies you can hear the most curious sound ever to come from a tree; it's like the passing of a little country train, very far in the distance, perhaps only in memory. Next the music is communicated to my wood of aspens and silver birches, about thirty of them together on the edge of a ravine. In this grove of young trees the wind suggests the trickling of a cool brook. Trickle, trickle, a young brook trickles steadily in my wood of birch and aspen.

Finally the instruments combine to take up the theme of triumphant summer. All is peace on such days, even though every form of plant life shakes, bows and dances about like a musician under the baton of an orchestra leader, even the grasses at the foot of the trees gone mad, running and running in place, without ever finding time to straighten up. The river in the misshapen willows, the faraway train among the pines, the swift brook on the edge of the ravine, all speak of a mysterious and secret accord.

On these days of full-throated music, my wild red

30

cherry tree, a quivering silhouette against the backdrop of the river, can scarcely make its muted song be heard.

So without contributing much to the symphony of the world, it sways at least to its own rhythm, all sails unfurled. With the black bird aboard and me in my garden chair, we spent many hours travelling together on the same wave of time.

III

But alas, Jeannot was growing old. He was becoming less prompt at extracting himself from scrapes. More than once I had heard a bullet whistle perilously close to him when he stopped off in passing to have a bite at Monsieur Simon's. I had told him to be careful, that misfortune would come from that side. But he was never one to take advice willingly from humans. Or from his own tribe either. He was a loner.

I was waiting for him one day in my place in the garden. The air stirred the leaves, the pine needles, the grasses. It was a day fashioned in every respect to delight Jeannot. Then through the vocal ensemble that at times so closely imitates the wind high in the sky, I thought I heard the dull sound of a shot. How anxious I felt as I scanned the unbroken blue of the sky. But then, what a relief, the familiar little shape appeared. I was about to laugh once more at the fruitless efforts of Monsieur Simon when—misfortune—the bird plunged towards the ground like a plane in distress. Oh little friend, I thought, at least don't fall on the road where car after car will run over your crushed body.

Jeannot exerted a surprising effort. Steadying himself more or less, he reached a current of air that carried him almost to my yard. Just before he managed it, however, he almost fell again, climbed clumsily, dragged himself, you might say, on his wings to a point just over the cherry tree. At that moment the air ceased almost all movement, as if to aid the wounded bird. His perch received him. Once again he dug in his claws. The gentle wind resumed and wafted him through the sky.

Then the little form at the heart of the tree collapsed, suddenly soft. Jeannot's attire of such beautiful black caught fire as a ray of sun pierced the foliage, making it shine between the branches like a polished coal.

At once the gulls announced high in the sky that Jeannot was dead. Though he had never stood with them in strange companionship on the exposed rocks when the tide rose or fell, nevertheless they were the first to mourn him.

"Jeannot is dead! Jeannot is dead!"

Thus the news reached a huge detachment of crows just returning from Baie-Saint-Paul. As one they continued their flight straight to Monsieur Simon's, crying, "He's the culprit! He's the one!"

Never have I seen so many birds rise up in so little time and from all sides at once. They came from the high fields between the village and the mountain ridge. They came from the more distant hollows behind that first ridge. They came from the fields below. And all converged upon Monsieur Simon's garden.

The poor man must have believed that the birds had gone mad and his last hour was at hand. Beating at the air with his hands, he ran here and there, shouting till he was breathless, "Go away! Go away!"

Far from going away, the birds inscribed great circles in the air, descending lower and lower to brush against Monsieur Simon. And they shouted at him in turn, "Caw caw! Shame and pity! To have killed Jeannot for a tomato!"

Finally they left a place now forever detestable in their sight. They flew to my house and circled round the small black shape in the branches, chanting the funeral service of Jeannot. At last the wind swept him to the ground. I asked Aimé to come then and together we dug a grave at the foot of the wild red cherry tree. Here Jeannot reposes.

And since that day the crows have never failed to call to me as they pass, "Caw, caw, caw!"

The Rover

Today Aimé's three cows are standing with their feet in the bit of a pond near my house. They are grazing on the flowers that encircle this speck of water—mostly swamp candles at this season. From time to time one leans down to taste the sun-warmed water, savouring it rather than drinking. Around her neck the Rover wears the bell Aimé rushed off to buy for her in Baie-Saint-Paul the day she stayed hidden for hours in the alders, refusing to show herself at his call.

"At least now I'll know where she is, the bitch."

Since then the bell has jingled at each of the bitch's movements and you always know where she is. Furthermore, the urge to hide seems to have left her now that the bell at her neck announces her presence wherever she goes.

Its tone is melodious, sweet and charming to hear.

If we're in one of our heavy calms, there is no other noise and the thin chime delights us. If there is wind, the sound can just be heard over the stirring of the leaves.

Sometimes it reaches us from so far away we feel that it comes from another time, another country.

Today the three cows are together. Feet in the water, they muse for long moments, their eyes scarcely raised from the ground, staring ahead without expression like many of the people I know when, without being quite aware of it, they follow some vague idea.

For, curiously, ever since the Rover has scattered music around her, the other two cows never leave her side. So when Aimé finds the Rover, he finds them also.

An instant ago all three came over to my fence, as if stirred by a sudden curiosity to know what I was doing.

The bell pealed loudly, very close. And why did it suddenly waken a memory—that I had believed dead—of the time in my childhood when I used to spend summer holidays with my uncles on their farms in Manitoba? The moment I left the train, I'd be greeted by the tinkling of the handbell with which the hotel keeper on his doorstep announced that a hot meal was ready ... and the sound would make me mysteriously happy as if we were being summoned, all of us strangers on the platform, to a splendid meal of festivity and friendship.

Because Aimé became exasperated with his cow and put a bell around her neck, I was given back this curious joy of my life, though even now I am not quite sure what it is made of or why it enchants me still.

36

Souls in Torment

Our killdeer is certainly the most nervous and apprehensive of living creatures. That is to say, he and his wife. For these two are as one. Just let Madame Killdeer weep and Monsieur Killdeer also weeps.

They chanced that summer to live not far from me near a bit of water beside the road. It wasn't a pond or even a pool, really no more than a puddle of rain and melted snow. Alders, a hundred times cut down, a hundred times grown up again, enclosed it with a low but bushy wall; it was this that retained the moisture.

Curiously enough, before it was a hollow, this puddle was a small pebbly elevation. A few years ago my neighbour Aimé began to remove gravel from it for the road or his own use. The result was this hole that is filled up each spring by the thawing snow and heavy rains. In summer the level falls but never sufficiently to uncover the bottom completely. There is always at least enough water to hold a mirror to the placid countryside around. And as the bottom is sandy and the water clean, the mirror offered to the serene sky and the new shoots of the alders remains limpid and reflects everything with perfect fidelity. The modest little spot, pretty in fact, is as pretty in its mirror.

And it became even prettier as all around the water there formed a border of flowers.

The first to appear, I believe, were the swamp candles. The wind helped their rather difficult migration from the damp meadow at the base of the hill to our narrow dry plateau, which till then held little attraction for them. But the appearance of this bit of water among the alders apparently changed everything. Swamp candles, for so long abundant in the lowlands, migrated in force so that there were soon enough of them to encircle the water with a fringe of delicate flowers of the most exquisite yellow. Or rather with two fringes, one erect and the other reversed in the water; and which was the most lifelike it would be difficult to say.

The next year came the flags. Some planted themselves squarely in the puddle; a good number remained timidly on shore, mingling their dreamy blue with the soft yellow of the swamp candles. But the reeds must have arrived even earlier for there were already a good hundred of them, a little sparse in places, in others tangled together.

Things had reached this point and the clear surface of the water with its double girdle of flowers and young reeds already looked like a sort of lake when one fine morning along came Madame Dragonfly, arrayed in tender blue, to revolve silently and continually in this tiny corner of the vast country.

More creatures than one might imagine like to live in peace around a lazy stretch of water that never flows. Frogs were present already with their tadpoles; also skater bugs, leaving momentarily on the surface the marks of their zig-zags; a spider too—all of them peaceable folk, good neighbours, whose natures were mar-

vellously in tune with the tranquillity of the surround-
ings.

But one day in May two travellers from Minnesota,
Monsieur and Madame Killdeer, descended upon us, and
the place lost forever the peace and harmony that had already won it renown in far-off corners of the land.

Scarcely had they arranged a sort of nest right on the
ground in the alder thicket, and scarcely had Madame
Killdeer laid four eggs, than she and Monsieur Killdeer
became frantic with apprehension.

"Don't come over here!" they screamed to all comers.
"Not over here! For pity's sake, keep your distance! Good
heavens, our poor eggs!"

Now the spot, despite its touch of wildness, was
much frequented. To the left lay the dirt road to the village. To the right was the private path, faintly traced
among the alders, that I used as a short cut to go a hundred times a day to visit my good neighbour Aimé.

Almost hourly someone passed this little corner that
the travellers from Minnesota must have staked out on a
calm day and expected to be just as calm from one end of
the year to the other.

Invariably the killdeers flew into a senseless panic.
Madame Killdeer rose above the cropped alders, sobbing
heartbrokenly.

"Kill-dee! Kill-dee! Go away! Go away, all of you!"

Monsieur Killdeer raced about madly on his long
thin legs, now to the right, now to the left, to make us believe the nest was anywhere but where it was.

"It's over here!" he lied. "It's over here!"

Meanwhile, not hearing what her husband was saying, Madame Killdeer shrieked just as loudly, "It's over
here! It's over here!"

And off she went in the opposite direction.

Of course no one believed either one of them. In any
event, there wasn't a human being among us who would

have dreamed for a moment of taking their eggs or, later, their poor little nestlings. Yet what a summer of misery we spent! Always on the alert. Always on the watch.

First there was the milkman, stopping as usual at the house near the puddle beside the road. Immediately out burst wild lamentations.

"It's over here ... over here ... !"

"No, not here ... not here ..."

"Here ... here ..."

There was an interval of silence. And since the fat green frog and her children, Madame Dragonfly and the spider never make a commotion, everyone rested for an instant.

Then the baker's van arrived.

Monsieur and Madame Killdeer ran senselessly, each to his own side, shrieking as if to drown out one another's voices.

"Over here! Over here!"

"Not true! It's over here! Over here!"

Our cheerful baker, who likes to chat from house to house, came out of Madame Maria's and stood for a good five minutes on the stoop, giving the news, his arms full of bread.

Insane with nervous tension, the killdeers cried in turn, then together, "That's enough! Enough! Quite enough talk!"

Our baker, who's as wholesome looking as his bread, finally stopped talking and departed. Madame Maria went back into her house. There was peace for ten minutes perhaps.

But soon up the hill streamed a band of village children, pails tinkling joyfully in their hands, on their way to pick raspberries. The pleasant metallic sound and the clear childish voices were lost in the eternal complaint.

"What are you going to do here? Here? Here?"

"Not here! Not here!"

It was enough to make you lose your mind.

When I myself ventured along my path a while later, I took great pains not to alarm the birds, which had just calmed down. I walked warily, not cracking any branches. No use, the small delicate ears of the killdeers caught my approach. They rose from a clump of alders, fluttering here and there as if this was the first time they'd seen a human being.

"Kill-dee!" one informed me almost intelligibly although I've never known what this could mean in killdeer language.

"Kill-dee," repeated the other firmly, then they took up their usual shrieks of "Over here!" and "Not here!"

I had time to examine them as they flew low around me. They were very handsome birds, as gifted for flight as for racing about on their long fragile legs. Clearly on their breasts they wore double collars of rich velvet-like black. But such incorrigibly anxious natures!

"With this disposition," I asked them one day, "why oh why did you come to live in such a travelled spot? Couldn't you find a better hiding place? Why here?"

"Kill-dee, kill-dee!" one replied. "It was this restful water that attracted us."

"There must be plenty elsewhere ... better hidden," I said.

"Kill-dee ... kill-dee ... There's no water anywhere as pure as this or as pretty. ... Now take yourself far from here ... here ..."

I couldn't get another word from them.

"At least," I said, "do try to profit from your mistake and next year seek elsewhere."

"Kill-dee," they said. "We won't come back here. Not here."

But a moment later I believe I caught, "Perhaps again here! Again here! Again here!"

The big emerald-green frog finally had enough of these comings and goings and the endless complaining. Of a cheerful nature herself, she was unable to understand how anyone could spend his whole life fearing the worst and seeing enemies on every hand. With forty of her children who were now old enough to hop after her from hollow to hollow, she emigrated to a rather dark and far less attractive pond that had at least the advantage of being wrapped in silence. And there she aged gently in a very short time, without losing any of her inclination to look on the bright side of things.

Meanwhile on our plateau the killdeers had reached a high pitch of nervous excitement. For it was now July and scouts had come to camp in the district. At all hours of the day they paraded past, singing at the top of their voices. In the evening, seated around their campfire, they sang again. As well, there was a constant stream of visitors at my neighbour's. Almost all the aunts came, then the nieces, then cousins and more cousins. I too had my share of company. To make matters worse, the village children raced tirelessly along our little road on their bicycles, all the dogs of the plateau at their heels, barking non-stop. This excited Aimé's cows, which began to run like mad creatures in their pasture adjoining the water. To describe the panic of the killdeers those days is almost impossible. Scarcely had they descended into the alder brush to comfort and reassure their children than they would take to the air again or dash across country. And they contradicted one another more than ever, so jittery now they no longer knew what they were saying.

"Kill-dee! Our nest isn't here! ... Not here!"

"Kill-dee! It's over here! ... Over here!"

And they ran hither and yon, one to the right, the other to the left, each denying what the other had said.

Surely they've finally learned their lesson, I told myself, and we'll never see them here again.

Monsieur Killdeer agreed, "Oh no! Never here! ... Never here!"

But Madame Killdeer, perhaps not catching what he had said or just contrary, insisted, "Well, yes! It will be here! For where would you suggest that we go?"

"No, I said not here!" I heard in the distance from poor Monsieur Killdeer, hoping to have the final word for once.

Then at last, having raised their children as best they could, Monsieur and Madame rose from their wretched hiding place one day with their four little killdeers. To fly directly to the South, with a brief stopover perhaps in Minnesota.

"Kill-dee!" they flung back, for once both saying the same thing. "It's all over ... all over ... all over ..."

And a silence such as we had not known for many months settled around the dreaming water.

Then, though we were on the brink of autumn, who do you think returned? Our emerald-green frog, delighted to be back in her original home now that it was peaceful again. She knew all its advantages, having tried another that was much less desirable. At one side of the water there was mud and here she dug herself a deep shelter for the winter, disappearing into it completely after one final look from her big bulging eyes at the world around.

The swamp candles and the flags died but they had entrusted their survival to the sodden earth, which preserved it. Likewise the reeds. Then the little pond seemed lifeless. From day to day the sky darkened. Would you believe me if I tell you that in the grey desolation that marks the approach of the harsh season, Berthe and I came to feel regret at no longer hearing the lamentation of the killdeers? Because it is akin to the anxiety of the human heart? That may be. But certainly something was missing.

In any event, it's well over, I told myself. We won't

see Monsieur and Madame Killdeer again. They've suffered so much misery amongst us, they'll never forget it.

Winter took hold. Our simple-minded frog slept without dreaming, deep under the ice. How the spider hibernated I don't quite know. Soon snow accumulated in the hollow beside the road. What had been, you remember, a pleasant semblance of a lake, almost oval in shape, became an insurmountable snow bank which the wind piled higher with each new storm.

Under the mild spring sun the snow yielded a great deal of water. The soil appeared, rejuvenated. Then, clear yellow, the family of swamp candles, twice as numerous as last year. Also the flags, perhaps the most pensive of all flowers. The alders, cut down in the fall, sprang up afresh, as determined to live as ever. In the centre the new water reflected sky, some small white clouds and from time to time the flight of a duck as with wings outstretched and harried expression he headed only he knew where.

But we mustn't forget to mention Madame Dragonfly, who had arrived a while ago. Just as the summer before, she kept circling about in the perfect little spot to which, I may say, she added the final graceful touch as she brushed the clumps of flags with her wings.

And then, believe it or not, in the midst of all this peace and harmony, as I was coming along my path through the alders one lovely June day, what did I hear?

"Don't come here! We have eggs! Keep your distance! Go away!"

"Over here! ... It's over here!"

"No! ... Not here! ... Not here!"

"Are you crazy?" I asked. "When you had the whole mountain to hide in. And the wild shore of the river beyond Cap Maillard. And the entire old seigneury of Monseigneur Laval. What came over you? Oh what came over you to return?"

Between two anxious cries, I thought I heard, "It was this lovely little bit of water, so calm ... the yellow flowers all around ... the sky in the water ..."

"And the blue flowers ... and the peace ..."

"... that drew us back ... kill-dee ... And even the people, who no longer frighten us very much ..."

"Almost not at all ..."

"Just a little still ..."

And in the sky I heard fear and happiness, dread and trust; and I said to myself, "These birds with the wavering hearts—they're you, they're me, they're all of us, children of this Earth."

A Mobile

Marcel found a family of daisies—about twenty—set at long intervals on a single supple stalk. Quite ordinary field daisies, white with clear yellow centres. What gave them their beauty was the graceful way they were scattered though still attached to the same source. He put them in a narrow-necked vase on a low table from which they projected far into the room. They were so slender and so delicate that a faint current of air set them quivering.

"A mobile of flowers," I congratulated my husband.

Mouffette, my little cat, jumped on the table. She tapped one of the flowers as she might have struck a note on a keyboard; all the flowers trembled. She reached for another higher up; the same result. Then Mouffette turned her head as if to say, "What a lovely toy!"

"Mouffette, no, stop," we protested. "In the whole summer we may never find another such keyboard of daisies."

One paw in the air, she was enjoying herself immensely. The game of the little black-and-white cat juggling with the quivering flowers was so graceful that we finally let her be.

I set this daisy a-shaking; nineteen other daisies vibrate. I try to stop the game; off they go wilder than ever.

Suspended from the tender daisies, paw now on one, now on another, Mouffette looked like a little carillonneur.

Long Skinny Minny

As everyone knows, cats are not very fond of going for walks with their masters. They prefer to wait for them to return, sitting on the stoop. Or perhaps on a window ledge, where they are in a good position to see within and without. It is said that they are more attached to places than to people though this is far from being proved. What is certain, however, is that they love their houses dearly. For proof you need only see them on the first brisk fall days, huddled shivering on the doorstep, fur standing on end, paws tucked in, waiting perhaps a whole day for their folks to get back from visiting in some distant concession. The icy wind may be blowing from that side. No matter. They want to wait as close to the doorstep as they can.

However, there are cats that do follow their masters, very few, but there are some. Like Grisou, a little blue-grey cat that spent its entire short life trying to accompany Aimé, my neighbour, when he went each day to the mountain to chop down trees.

In the still shimmering dawn Aimé would set out

along the rough path on foot. Regretfully leaving his cosy nook behind the stove, Grisou would once again manage to leave at his heels without being observed. Confronted with the huge frigid outdoors, he would hesitate for a moment, meowing with fear and shock, yet still not losing sight of Aimé striding ahead. The freshly fallen snow often engulfed the little cat to his eyes. He would extricate himself with an effort and catch up with his master, then rub against Aimé's leg in contentment, wasting his energy trying to purr. So that once again he was left behind. He would try to find short cuts, plunge into the soft snow once more, call for help, mewing desperately, overtake his master again and lose him again and finally sit down, very small and frightened, wailing among the great dark tree trunks. At this Aimé, who'd hoped to exhaust the patience of the little cat and force him to return home, would retrace his steps, take poor cold-stiffened Grisou and set him on his shoulder. Together the two would continue the ascent, Aimé's breath in a white cloud, the little cat clinging with all his claws to his master's woollen jacket. Even so he would appear to be dancing on Aimé's shoulder as it rose and fell with the rhythm of the walk. And as soon as the terrain became smoother and the cat's equilibrium more secure, he would begin to purr in his master's ear.

"Crazy little fool," Aimé would say. "When will you learn to stay home?"

This was quite an exceptional case among cats and, if I've described it, that was only to show the difference between Grisou and, for instance, his own mother, who was as stay-at-home a beast as you could find.

Called Long Skinny Minny, she was not in the least handsome. A scrawny attenuated cat with a crooked tail, she had irregular splotches of bluish grey scattered haphazardly over her white fur, which I must in fairness say she kept scrupulously clean.

By nature she was sullen, morose, stubborn and always fidgety.

Either she was about to have kittens and was turning over her old hiding places in her mind, those that had succeeded and those that had been discovered, with an air of complete distraction as she asked herself, "Are the oldest ones now sufficiently old to be safe to use again? Or would it be better to find one that was brand new?" But she had already had almost sixty offspring. The farm was running out of secure places for the first days of the kittens. Once their eyes were open, they were safe: too cute to be disposed of.

Or if she wasn't about to produce a litter, she'd just had one. But she'd be as distrustful as ever, taking a new complicated way to her hiding place each time. So that she sometimes became completely muddled and lost her way.

However—how strange was the nature of that cat—the moment her kittens were able to fend for themselves, she again took her place firmly among the humans. Henceforth the single thought in her head was to live in the house with the people, installed among them in the best chair, lending an ear to all conversations. And she was constantly at one door or another, begging to be let in.

Now Berthe and her brother Aimé have a strict rule: in summer cats are best outdoors. So they are not readily admitted to the house.

Scarcely had Long Skinny Minny contrived to sneak into the kitchen on someone's heels than she would find herself unceremoniously back outside. No matter. She would hear Aimé coming from the barn with the milk pails. Immediately she was at the back door and had managed to get in, Aimé having no free hand to prevent her. If he tried to bar her way with his foot, she vaulted it easily.

"The cat's in again, put her out," Berthe would say,

busy frying a pan of salmon trout or slices of bread soaked in maple syrup.

Naturally it was at the most enticing hour that Long Skinny Minny always deployed all her efforts to reach the kitchen. In the bustle of supper hour with everyone occupied, she more than once succeeded in leaping onto the table and devouring an entire trout right under our noses before we could recover from our surprise enough to shout, "Shoo! Thief!" which didn't disconcert her in the least.

"That cat has no pride," Berthe decided one day.

Seated rocking while everything was being made ready, I went somewhat mildly to the defence of the cat.

"She may be hungry."

"I've just fed her the heads and guts of the fish," said Berthe. "Scat! Out!"

And she dispatched the cat outdoors.

As we were on the point of sitting down to eat, in came the baker and Long Skinny Minny entered triumphantly behind him since he hadn't thought to slam the door in her face.

He sat down. She also.

Two minutes later Berthe accompanied the baker to his van to choose some cakes and took the opportunity to put the cat back out, and the cat took the opportunity of Berthe's return with loaded arms to enter anew.

She eventually wore people down. Aime's house is lively with many visitors. In the course of a single evening I've seen the cat put to the door twenty or even thirty times. Towards eleven o'clock it was not unusual to see her ensconced in the best chair, pretending to be asleep. From time to time she would open her eyes and bestow upon the company a strange glance in which there was less friendliness than a stubborn need, I think, to establish her importance and her place among us.

Nowhere in the world, I imagine, was there a more

stay-at-home-and-sit-by-the-fire cat than this. Unlike Tontine, the little dog of the household, who went into a frenzy of joy whenever she was invited to go for a walk, Long Skinny Minny on her cushion always seemed eager to see us depart. Stretching indolently from head to toes, she would toss us a queer look, at once detached and a shade impatient, as if she were saying, "Why can't you be off then? It's never so nice as when the masters are out and you have the house to yourself."

No doubt it must also have been pleasant for her to be free for an hour or so from the perpetual humiliations and insults of that detestable Tontine.

Be that as it may, this cat, hitherto so set in her ways, finally did something one day that she had never done before and thus dumbfounded us completely.

Berthe and I were getting ready that day to go down to the river to fish for tommycod and Tontine was dancing around, beside herself with joy, giving piercing cries, "Yes! Yes! Let's go down to the river! Let's hurry!"

The small dog with the long reddish fur, half mongrel, half Pekinese, was so passionately fond of going down to the river that she'd learned to recognize the word. If we as much as uttered it in conversation, even though Tontine seemed to be sound asleep, she would immediately open her eyes, lift her head and half rise, already excited by the hope of going with us.

But why she so doted upon going down to the river remained puzzling. For once she'd reached its banks, she didn't even look at the water. Nor did she listen to what was for Berthe and me an inexhaustible joy: the infinite sound of the waves, forever dispersing, forever gathering themselves together again. And she certainly never went swimming but was careful to recoil sharply when, some time after the passage of a ship, a long wave broke unexpectedly on the shore. Moreover, she never went down there on her own as she might have done a hundred times a day. I decided finally that it was seeing us, human beings, made happy by this surprising expanse of water that in the end won over the little dog. "Since they like it so much," she perhaps said to herself, "let's give it a try too." For she had a warm heart, though dreadfully jealous.

So as we had been on our way for several minutes, we suddenly observed Long Skinny Minny trying to follow us and already entangled in the long grass. She must have managed to sneak out behind us without being noticed as she'd managed to sneak in a thousand times.

"This is a surprise," I said. "What's come over her?"

"She's getting old," said Berthe. "And when she's expecting kittens now, you'd think she no longer knows what she wants—to stay or follow, be with people or alone."

And she called over her shoulder to the cat, "You'd better go back to the house. It's too far for you."

That was a mistake, for Tontine had also turned and had seen the cat, who at once flattened herself in the grass, trying to disappear. Tontine raced up the hill like a meteor and repeated the advice in her own way, eyes furious, lip drawn back. For once Long Skinny Minny seemed about to turn on her old enemy. She spat three or four times in Tontine's face. Caught for a moment between these deplorable manners and Berthe's remonstrances, "Ah, bad girl! Come here, bad girl!" Tontine eventually obeyed and returned to our side.

But snarling still, she threatened in an undertone, "Just as long as she doesn't come any closer, for then I promise nothing."

After a moment we saw that Long Skinny Minny was still following us but at a distance, ready to flatten herself in the grass as soon as Tontine glanced in her direction.

54

"Between the slinking cat and the growls of the dog, we're going to have a cheerful walk," I said.

Berthe also seemed disappointed. But she said with a sort of compassion, "It's pitiful just the same."

And she tried again, gently, to send the cat back.

"You'd be much better off at home. Go on. Go home."

Halfway up the hill the head of the cat, scarcely higher than the grass, shook in negation, rather sadly.

We found it inexplicable that Long Skinny Minny should apparently be every bit as attached to us today as she had previously been to the house.

"You'd think she was afraid to be alone these days," said Berthe. "And as for getting her to change her mind, if she's taken a notion to follow us, you might as well try to move the mountain."

So we went on, more or less together, a drawn-out line with Long Skinny Minny far at the rear.

But matters became even worse. For to reach the river you have to go down a steep hill. Great rocks pierce the surface, which is rough and uneven at best. In spots the path is dry, in others always wet. You need to be appropriately shod. Long Skinny Minny kept cutting her paws on the sharp edges of the rock. She got them wet in the damp places, which seemed to displease her even more for she kept drawing one or other of them from the water and shaking it vigorously. At intervals the poor creature sat down to lick the tender cushions of her injured paws. With a helpless look she inquired of us, whimpering, "Couldn't you at least slow down? You know perfectly well I'm not wearing good heavy shoes like you."

Tontine, still nursing her rancour, raced up at once to laugh in her face.

"What came over you to decide to follow us to the river? The river isn't for you. Now put up with it."

Berthe and I finally sat down to enable Long Skinny

Minny to rest for a while. Clearly the harder the way became, the less she would consent to give up. It was as if she were trying to tell us with her big eyes, so full of fatigue and stubbornness, "Do you folks think now that I've managed all this difficult bit I have any intention of returning?"

Tontine made a detour and sat down some distance from the cat, ostentatiously turning her back. And she gave a great sigh of repressed ill-temper.

The place where we were sitting is leafy and shadowy: a narrow clearing between the tangled alders and a few birch trees whose white bark relieves this slightly too sombre wood. We had seated ourselves on a smooth rock and in some connection that escapes me now began to talk about life, how it changes as we advance, as we ourselves change, how hard it is at times to find ourselves again.

Already we could hear, rather faintly, the beating of the water against the shore and the sound became linked with what we were saying. The river and life, both in motion, seemed very close to one another, though the movement of the river soothes us and life often gives us pain as we try to follow it.

"When I was a child," Berthe told me, "my mother used to send me to the spring in this wood with butter, milk and cream. Now we have a refrigerator to keep things cool. It's a thousand times more convenient but we've lost the pleasure of the spring."

"Where is it?" I asked.

She showed me. We uncovered it under some tall dark-green ferns. It made only a tiny sound, scarcely louder than that of the hand of a clock marking the time. It was gentle and enigmatic, as mysterious as at the beginning of its life.

"It's years since I've seen it," said Berthe. "Now that we don't need it any more."

56

Leaning over the water, we could see very dimly our own darkened faces.

"You can only wonder," I said, "whether what we gain in living is worth what is lost."

At this Tontine, her muzzle flat on the ground but her eyes wide open and her ears impatient, barked briefly as if trying to say, "Do stop talking about life. What's the use? What can you change? Come on, let's get down to the river."

But Long Skinny Minny appeared happy to hear us speaking about the difficulties of living with ourselves and with others. She was lying on her side, still panting slightly, and from time to time she half opened her eyes to give us a golden look that was beginning to grow peaceful.

"That's it," she seemed to be saying. "Talk about life, which is hard to understand and hard to live."

And she turned to Tontine a face of stone.

When we had all four rested, we resumed our descent. The cat lamented less. Doubtless she thought the roughest part of the journey was over and she had a chance of seeing the end. But as if to taunt her by showing how easy the path was for anyone who had the hang of it, Tontine had taken to a cruel game. She raced up the hill and down just as quickly, then raced up again, each time circling the cat, yapping. With more dignity than one would have believed possible, Long Skinny Minny no longer spat or even answered this provocation but simply withdrew a single step from the brazen Tontine.

Then we came out onto the beach with its scattering of great rocks. Beyond lay the accustomed splendour of the river—to which, however, one never grows accustomed. For the thousandth time it gripped our hearts. At the same time the murmuring of the water, the most ancient song of Earth, welcomed and enfolded us. Tontine gave us a knowing look, assuring herself that it was the same as on all the other occasions, we were already solaced. Then she found herself a nice dry spot behind one of the boulders, turned in a circle and lay down with another sigh, this time of relief.

"At last you'll be quiet for a moment. I'll avail myself of the opportunity to have a rest myself," she told us with a look in which all her concern for us was gradually borne away by a need for sleep.

A little higher up the cat stretched to her full length, scrawny everywhere except for her almost constantly swollen belly. She cast a vague, somewhat bored look at all that water stretching into infinity. What a detestable element! And to think there are people who'll go right to the edge of it—or into it even! She panted gently, composing herself after the emotions of the journey, then she too closed her eyes.

For Berthe and for me, time was of little account, we scarcely see it pass when we are beside the river. It drifts into the song of the tide, which rises and falls, almost the same always. The eternal has seemingly no need to change. To our animal friends also time doesn't seem long near the water, provided we are with them. While we dream, released and marvellously free, they sleep, their minds finally reassured on our account.

Why then did I suddenly break the spell that day by suggesting, "Berthe, suppose we walk along the track?"

Tontine rose to go with us, resigned to follow because she must, but with a rather cross expression.

"What a notion, when we're so comfortable here in the cool, to seek misery elsewhere! How like that curious friend of my mistress who's never happy anywhere for long."

As for Long Skinny Minny, she looked utterly horror-stricken. "What sort of surface will I find there for my already sorely tried paws? And what's the track? Why are they now talking about such an unheard-of place?"

To tell the truth, with her crooked tail, her frantic expression, the amazement in her eyes at wakening here beside the water, she looked crazier than ever.

Yet—what else could she do once launched upon such a foolhardy escapade—she went a little way back with us. There, on a narrow bit of level ground parallel to the river, lies the railroad track.

Berthe and I moved haltingly over the ties, which are set irregularly, as if to discourage people from walking there. The body quickly becomes weary. However, the spirit rejoices, as if it imagined itself freer here than on the road of everyone else.

We had covered a fair bit of ground before we noticed that our animals were—as the saying goes—dragging their feet. Even for Tontine the rough ballast was painful. She was walking like an arthritic with short steps, head down, but without complaint. You have to give Tontine her due, she's not a whiner. But Long Skinny Minny, seated between the rails, eyes bewildered, looked as if she were on the point of giving up but, perhaps not remembering the way or simply too tired to go in either direction, she lamented at the top of her lungs.

"Where have we got to now? Where are we going? Where can it lead, a road like this? Oh why didn't anyone tell me we were going to the back of beyond?"

Tontine gave her a brief glance and a brief growl.

"We did tell you. If you don't like it here, go back. It's hard enough on this road as it is without having to listen to your doleful wails as well."

Poor Long Skinny Minny. To think that she was about to demonstrate a rare and unsuspected talent just when we, in our ignorance, thinking her too stupid, were ready to turn back. But happily I became a child again and had an impulse to try to walk on a single rail, as I used to do when I was seven or eight.

Arms extended to either side for balance, I at first

managed only six or seven steps. I got back and did a little better. Still nothing brilliant. Berthe passed me on the other rail. I began to feel jealous. We then joined hands across the roadbed, trying to support one another. In a moment we were laughing. Life suddenly seemed tender, comic, amusing. Were two slim little girls who had run nimbly along the rail looking at us across the years with a touch of pity? The dog and cat were astonished, in any case. Tontine, who had never seen her mistress give way to such whimsy, was dumbfounded. And as always when she can no longer understand the actions of those she loves, she was whimpering. However, Long Skinny Minny, seated again between the rails but not wailing any more, was watching us, her small narrow face now all attention, all shrewdness, all intelligence.

And suddenly she took off. She passed us easily, tail held high. That perfectly erect tail gave her an entirely new personality. Never would I have thought that the mere angle of a tail could make such a difference.

A short distance ahead of us she jumped onto the rail and continued along at the same speed, tail still high and straight. She didn't even waver but proceeded as if it were nothing. Then, without slowing down, she tossed us a look over her shoulder.

"So this is what you find so difficult! But it's perfectly simple!"

We were thunderstruck. She went on at her ease. A nice firm little trot that never varied. And all this time her head assured, ears erect, tail high.

"That's marvellous!" we congratulated her. "No one on earth is better at running the rail."

Modestly, as if not to claim more than her due, she granted us a brief glance that said, "Ah, that's because you have such wide feet and, poor souls, you only have two."

Despite her unassuming air, we could see that she was rather proud of herself.

The one who looked small at this moment was Tontine.

One ear drooping, tail brushing the ground, an expression of complete incredulity on her face, she watched her bitter enemy continue on her way with such sovereign ease. She gave sighs of envy and grief that reached their height when, without thought for Tontine's feelings, we once more congratulated the cat, "Bravo! Bravo!"

Then Tontine committed the folly of follies. She pulled herself onto the rail and immediately fell off. Obstinately she tried again and with great difficulty achieved four heavy hesitant steps.

The polished steel provided no purchase for her clumsy claws. The poor stubborn creature teetered and landed on her back.

The sole comment of the cat, which had all the cards in hand for a magnificent revenge, was a sort of shrug. She was still running along ahead of us, with an occasional look behind that said mockingly, "Are you still hale and hearty? Shall we go as far as the eel fishing at l'Abatis? To Sault-au-Cochon?"

She seemed suddenly to know the whole region, its peculiarities, its geography.

"Or even to Petit Cap at the bottom of the old seigneury? How long is it now that I've heard you say you'd go there on foot one of these days?"

We had to call her back. Drunk with her success, she was capable of leading us right to Quebec. At first she played deaf and wouldn't even hear of leaving the rail. But when she saw us already halfway up the hill, she decided to return.

No doubt it was not so much running on the rail that intoxicated her as the fact that she'd astonished us. For she had further prowess to display.

In three bounds she ascended the steep hill, stomach on the ground, tail in a straight line with her nose.

At the top, however, she had the good grace to wait for us. There she sat with her tail wrapped around her paws, gazing at the river, the clouds and, far away, between blinks of her eyes, our little procession laboriously climbing.

And on her features was that vaguely amiable expression that comes to people as to animals when for once in their lives they have been admired.

The Tree Brothers

It was a mild summer day. Three crows on their way
to Grande-Pointe settled in the branches of the two
aspens beside the road near our house. I call them the
twins for never have two little trees growing side by side
resembled one another so closely: same height, same
slimness of body, same distribution of foliage, same
slightly timid way of holding themselves, so character-
istic of aspens—the least haughty of trees—yet perfectly
straight and enveloped in their own subdued music. All
day long they can be heard. If one is silent, it is only to
permit the other to speak. But usually they murmur together, both saying the same thing. Seeing the two of
them, issues apparently of the same stock, their foliage
intermingled, so close to one another that only a thread
of light can pass between them, you might believe they
had come into the world with the sole aim of mutual
support.

They stand at the edge of the road, just this side of
the old snake fence that Aimé patches up spring after
spring. A little farther and they would be right on the

road. So you cannot miss them, singing together, growing in the same proportion every year, touching in their similarity. Yet no one ever spoke of them. No one as much as hinted that he'd noticed them. Except the crows. For this wasn't the first time I'd seen some of them stop in the branches of the young aspens. And though at first I might have believed this a matter of convenience, I came to realize that they simply liked to perch in the little trees.

Two side by side on the same branch, the third facing them on a branch of the twin, the three crows began to converse beak to beak.

In my swing behind the cedar hedge I cannot be seen from the road but I have a fairly good view through its gaps of everything that passes by. Furthermore, I am in the best possible position to listen.

My three crows, who believed themselves completely alone, were chatting familiarly together. It was apparently the oldest that did most of the talking, the other two confining themselves to an occasional "Aah, Aah." And nothing could more resemble a peaceful conversation.

Even their "Caw caw" was not noisy and irritating today as it is when they themselves are irritated—if, for instance, one of their kind is being pursued or insults are hurled from earth into the sky, "Thieves! Robbers!"

Up from the village came a troop of little boys—not bad children usually but suddenly one of them picked up a stone from the gravel beside the road and flung it at the birds, shouting, "Ugly old things! Ugly old things!"

Two others followed suit.

Surprised, the crows were silent. As if slow to understand, they looked down at their feet without stirring. Then they rose from the branches and flew towards the wooded mountain, trailing their wings regretfully, three small black shapes that in the unfurled blue of today's sky suddenly struck a note of reproach.

The children mocked them, "Caw! Caw!" then went on their way.

In the renewed silence I heard the sighing of the two little trees just this side of the old rail fence.

Then half an hour later, all being calm again, the three crows returned and took up their former positions in the aspens, two on the same branch, their comrade opposite. And back they went to their conversation without the slightest hint in their stance or tone of voice that they were holding a grudge.

Yet crows are far from stupid. And they have memory to burn.

Then, announced by what you might call a mechanical shriek of agony, a truck with belly full of oil toiled slowly up the hill that leads to our peaceful plateau. The scents among which we live without always being aware of them—the smell, at once healthy and slightly rotten, of the tide; that of the sweet vernal-grass hidden by the brook; of clover too; and, when the wind is favourable, of old-fashioned roses around the roadside cross—all these delicate scents were drowned in the strong sickening reek of heating oil.

The crows didn't need to be told twice. If there is anything that will persuade them to take wing it is surely what we used to call impure air and now refer to as pollution.

The B.O. oil truck had scarcely reached the top of the slope when my three crows flew swiftly across the little meadow at the foot of the mountain, protesting with all their might, "Faugh! Faugh!"

And in the distance I seemed to hear them lament, "What shall we do? Will lack of air finally separate us from each other, the people and the birds? They in their village? We in the mountain? It will be sad. Heartbreaking."

"Heartbreaking," the little trees replied with a single voice.

"Heartbreaking," a robin seemed to agree with nods of the head as he busied himself searching for food in the grass nearby, and he gave me an incisive sidelong look.

The three crows must have been just as fond as I am of the two slender aspens, which are so united always that no one has ever heard them contradict one another. Or perhaps what they liked was their place in the branches, so convenient for seeing everything that comes along the road where, in their opinion, the good may outweigh the bad.

At any rate, they were soon back but now all lined up on a single branch, as if in a box at the opera, and not uttering a word.

Then from the direction of Grande-Pointe floated another pungent smell, this time not wholly disagreeable. It was the smell of the strong coarse tobacco smoked of old in the country districts. In an enclosed room it might be trying but mingled with the sea breeze it is not unpleasant. Soon I could see Wilbrod the Simple, the only one in the neighbourhood who still smokes this coarse tobacco of former times. He approached, wearing his checked bush shirt and lumberman's boots, his wide-bowled pipe in his mouth, his big scythe over his shoulder and a whetstone protruding from the back pocket of his trousers. He had been hired to hand-scythe the little bits of fields where the machine cannot pass—the specialty as it were of Wilbrod the Simple, he having also acquired one since everyone around him is now mechanized.

With his usual habit of announcing to himself out loud what he has to do, I heard him telling himself pleasantly, "You're going to clean up the apple orchard at Aimé's. Then you'll go home and milk the cow. Then you'll wash yourself all over . . ."

Through a hole in the hedge I saw him stop short at sight of the three crows, immobile, listening. At once his ancient face lit up with delight. He set his scythe blade-down on the ground and leaned on it as if on a cane. Despite the cloud of tobacco smoke that struck them full in the faces, the birds didn't even move. Wilbrod, head raised to look at them, began to address them very gently.

"Pretty little ladies. Pretty little crows. Sweet young ladies."

Immediately you would have said that the birds came as close to the road as they could with a sort of sliding of their bodies. The brilliant eyes of all three were fixed upon Wilbrod.

"My, they're smart," he said. "They see everything. Understand everything."

The crows inclined their heads slightly to the side for a better view through the leaves of this curious man who seemed to know whereof he spoke. The aspens quivered with the passage of a light breeze.

Wilbrod, arm resting on his scythe, asked the birds, "What do they think? Yes, what can they think? Of us? Of our world?"

When his young ladies made no reply, he said in farewell, "Smart little things. Smart as paint."

Then he departed, his scythe over his shoulder, puffing from his pipe almost as much smoke as rises in spring from maple-sugar shacks.

On the branch, imperceptibly, the three little black shapes had moved again to follow Wilbrod the Simple with their eyes. And they listened, beaks pointed, in the most attentive silence, as he informed himself, "Then you'll wash all over. Then you'll change your underwear. Then you'll say your prayers ..."

And the tree brothers replied in the same breath, "So be it."

The Festival
of the Cows

Today the cows are resting. All three lying down, their calves too. With nothing to do but let the warm wind rid them of flies, horseflies and gadflies. It was the first time I'd seen such a thing: in broad daylight, hooves tucked under them, all turned to receive this blessed wind between their horns, letting themselves live. Until now I'd never seen them when they weren't scratching themselves, first with one foot, then another, tails revolving, ears twitching, always in a state of defence against the torturing insects. I'd come to the conclusion that it was natural for them to sleep two minutes here, ten minutes there, and to live and die, as it were, on their feet.

As I cut through the field where they lay so perfectly at ease, I took care not to disturb them or force them to get up.

None of them rose as I passed but each one greeted me vaguely from somewhere deep within her eyes. They appeared to recognize me at first glance today. Because the dry wind had cleared their brains? Perhaps. But perhaps also because of my little white hat. I've noticed that

69

they seem to recognize me more quickly when they see it appear through the alders. Always, however, with a certain stupefaction, as if they were asking themselves, "When on earth is she going to buy herself another hat?"

Now what they do not know is that I buy a new hat every summer, identical always to the old one.

I zig-zagged between them, then, so as to disturb them as little as possible. I could hear their quiet breathing. Perhaps to savour this day that was unparallelled in their lives, they weren't even ruminating. With their big pleasant eyes they were saying, "We're at ease. What more do you want us to say? We're at ease. Today is the festival of the cows."

If they were still moving their tails gently, it was, one would say, as dogs do, simply to show their contentment.

One, two, at most three days of well-being in the whole summer, I told myself, and see how happy they are!

In fact, with their huge placid eyes, faces in the wind, backs to the river, they seemed to be thanking heaven that they'd come into the world as cows.

Not in the least stupid, moreover, they were lying on the highest point of the field where the air circulates most freely. Then, to enjoy the wind even more, they dug their noses into it and closed their eyes.

I arrived at Berthe's almost in a state of jubilation.

"Berthe! Berthe! Berthe!"

She was coming down the steep stairs from the attic. I didn't notice at first that she looked a little tired.

"Berthe, the cows are lying down. All resting. It's the festival of the cows!"

I saw then that she seemed concerned.

"What is it, Berthe?" But full of my subject, I didn't wait for her reply. "Cows happy to be cows, Berthe! Have you ever seen such a thing?"

"Oh, if all our friends were as happy," she said in a tone of slight reproach.

And she led me to the flower garden, which in my haste I hadn't stopped off to admire first thing as I usually do.

Everything had suffered here. The poppies hung down, their faces faded; many of the lupines were broken; the roses were shrivelled, the delphiniums shattered. Only a few of the strong dahlias held their ground though barely.

"It's this wind," Berthe said. "It's broken them all. I put up wind-breaks but you'd need a separate one for each flower."

I helped her erect others. From time to time I glanced towards the cows. On their hummock at the end of the field, in relief against the sky, they presented a rare picture of contentment. Or perhaps, now that the wind was in their favour, of egotism. They were certainly indifference itself as they watched us trying to rescue the flower garden.

"Well, what would you? For so long, every day has been the festival of the flowers. Today it's our turn." And they thrust their noses back into the wind. "Oh, how delicious!"

The Pair

E verything alive wants to live as one of a pair. Needs his counterpart. Or lacking a counterpart, some other creature.

Aimé's horse was obliged to live much of his life alone of his species. That is why he joined forces with the cows.

He spent the winters with them in the same little stable and the summers in the same pasture.

In summer he wasn't entirely with them. The cows formed their own compact small group and he stood some distance away—but never very far.

When the cows took a notion to descend the steep hill and seek cover in the alder brush, Prince went down also. (Between ourselves, this Prince led a rather menial life: bringing in the hay, transporting maple sap, hauling wood from the mountain.) The animals sometimes spent part of a week below, most of the time invisible. The day the cows returned, up came Prince at their heels.

Prince's attachment to the cows didn't become fully apparent to us, however, till the day Aimé decided to put him by himself for a while in a field across the road. He'd be much better off there, with grass that hadn't been browsed all summer, fine trees for shade, even a brook.

Yet he stood unmoving at the fence, gazing across the road at the cows. He called to them, whinnying. Or perhaps he was calling for his master to release him, who knows? All that day he neither ate nor drank. And there is every indication that he didn't sleep either.

Then the next day this horse, hitherto so gentle, began to lash out at the fence with his hooves and to fling himself against it so violently that he was considerably injured after a few hours. That night he managed to smash the fence down and at daybreak he was in his customary place near the cows on the knoll overlooking the river. And he was browsing with pleasure on the scanty grass of this wretched field that had already been browsed a hundred times.

Days when the cows suffered cruelly from the stings of no-see-ums and black flies, he suffered patiently at their side.

Days of rest, he rested with them.

After some time Aimé made another attempt to put Prince by himself. This time the horse leaped the fence almost at once and was back with the cows the same day.

Here and there, the animals still had a few days' relief. Then all four stood in the wind, the cows in the lead, the old horse bringing up the rear.

In these periods of respite the cows seemed more than ever to lose themselves in indolent daydreams that were reflected in their placid gaze.

But in the great agitated eyes of the horse there was still a shadow, a distant sorrow, perhaps the vague recollection of a lost happiness.

The horse was for so long a wild animal and may remember his freedom still.

* * *

74

But before the onset of the bad weather, Prince experienced a joy such as he had never known in all his life. A certain Adélard Dufour of the village was obliged to be away for a few weeks and brought his horse to board at Aimé's.

Aimé led it into the cow pasture.

Prince approached to meet the newcomer. The newcomer greeted him. Immediately they were friends.

Yet they had nothing in common except being horses. Flick was a pretty little white beast of very mild disposition that had almost never worked except to bring in a bit of hay each summer for his own cow, which was deeply attached to him and must miss him a great deal these days. Prince was an old roan, worn out by the hard transport of wood in winter on a steep snow-covered mountain road.

No matter, for as long as they were in the same pasture, they never left one another. They formed their own group. They were a pair. They stood together, heads crossed over the fence along the road. Here Flick had stationed himself as soon as he arrived, as if already watching for his master's return.

Prince joined him there, laying his neck on the neck of the little horse in consolation.

Since then they had spent hours, the neck of one on the neck of the other, silhouetted against the sky. If there were flies, they defended themselves with the same movement of tail and ears.

Their manes undulated similarly in the wind.

And shadow, sorrow, perhaps even memory too, had almost disappeared from their huge eyes.

Dance, Mouffette!

For three days my mischievous little cat hadn't thought of any new tricks to make me laugh or scold. Her hiding places had all been discovered, to Mouffette's considerable vexation.

First there was the one on top of the buffet. This is a mastodon of a piece, which almost touches the ceiling. Came the time to put Mouffette to bed in her basket in the kitchen. I called her; no answer. Of course it is always just before bedtime that she looks for a place to hide, as though she were saying, "If I have to be shut up, at least let me choose where."

I searched under the beds, in the cupboards, behind the chairs and the sofa. Without being very big, Mouffette at four months is quite easily spotted even at night, thanks to her white costume with black stripes.

Finally there was nowhere left to look except on top of the buffet. What gave me the idea was that I'd noticed a possible way to get up there: several book shelves first, then a catalogne rug on the wall, finally a bit of bare wall —a mere nothing to one who has good claws!

I placed a chair on the table and climbed up. There, squeezed against the ceiling, stretched out rather absurdly the better to escape unobserved, lay Mouffette, not in the least annoyed at being caught. Quite the contrary, she gave me a sort of wink that seemed to signify, "Ha ha! Fooled you that time, eh?"

Then she yawned, rose and seated herself at the extreme end of the buffet, which overlooks a bay window facing the sea. The little cat gazed into the distant water and assumed a look of contemplation as if to indicate that she'd climbed so high expressly to have a good overall view. And there is little doubt that, far above people and furniture, she must have enjoyed a unique panorama. At any rate, she was so content there that only hunger could bring her down.

The very next night Mouffette found another hiding place. Never the same one twice! This time she managed to slide under the tightly drawn bedspread without making a single wrinkle. In other words, lie invisibly in a made-up bed. She was so flat that I passed that way a good twenty times and didn't notice even the tiniest bulge or the least pucker. The twenty-first time a slight movement of breathing that barely lifted the bedspread caught my eye. I whipped off the spread. Discovered, Mouffette looked enchanted. She spends her time hunting for hiding places and yet she'd be bitterly disappointed if I didn't find her.

But hiding places were running out. There are limits to those you can be sure of in a small country house when, in addition, you have a mistress well versed in the trickery of young cats.

So after the bedspread caper, Mouffette became bored. There was no use my offering her favourite toys: a spool of thread, the balls of newspaper with which she plays hockey, even the big grocery bags she promenades about the room, hidden inside so that they seem to be walking across the floor on their own; I presented all these to no avail. Mouffette just complained with a sad meow, "It was much more fun when you used to hunt for me for hours, turning the house upside down while I played dead."

And the little demon, so full of tricks, yawned in my face. I have never ceased to be amazed that such a small creature can yawn so enormously. For several minutes, ideas failing her, she looked as if she didn't find life at all amusing.

Until yesterday evening. Yesterday evening there were no-see-ums. These are nasty insects, invisible to the naked eye, that sting ferociously. If there is light in the room, they go right through the screens and harass you in your bed. So I didn't put on the lights. Just an old oil lamp that I keep in case of power failure. Also a few citronella candles. So in the night infested with no-see-ums, I was as if in a fortress, protected by my counter-fires.

I sat in the gentle glimmering that seemed to make me even more aware than usual of the old wardrobe, the ancient chest that looks as if it came from a pirate ship, the tall well-waxed buffet, the prints on the walls. Mouffette too must have felt pacified. She jumped on my knees and examined my eyes at length by the flame of a candle. And I myself believed that I could see her great semi-phosphorescent eyes more clearly than ever before.

Then some friends arrived. I wanted to put on the lights.

They begged me not to.

"It's so much more pleasant to sit by candlelight."

"We haven't had the opportunity for such ages."

We discovered once more that sitting by candlelight, the door open to let the faint sounds of the night unobtrusively enter, is one of the wonders of life in the country.

Voices at once become softer, melting, as it were,

into the half-light. No one tries to drown out anyone else or talks non-stop, as if the chance to speak once lost would be gone forever. Each voice comes in its turn, measured and slow, broken by silences that are full of meaning. Coming from the heart, each voice seeks the heart.

And in the gentle glimmering, eyes often take on the quality of a dream. You might think they were tiny lakes, enclosed in darkness, illuminated by the far-off rays of some invisible light.

Fascinated, Mouffette went from one to the other of us, jumped onto the knees of this one, then that one, looked into our eyes in turn and suddenly tried to capture the glow with her paw.

Everyone flattered her, telling her she was the prettiest cat in the world, which Mouffette never tires of hearing. This little animal heart has just as much need as any human heart to know that it is loved.

Suddenly as she passed through the flickering of a candle, Mouffette caught sight of her misshapen shadow. Was she afraid? Or had she already grasped the comic possibilities of the situation?

Whichever it was, she played the broncho. Head down, neck twisted to look at us askance, back arched, tail likewise, she leaped high into the air in a series of bounds to the side, always presenting that menacing profile.

We laughed heartily to see this amicable little beast transformed into a dangerous animal.

No doubt our gaiety intoxicated Mouffette. The little fool was now playing at frightening herself.

"Dance, Mouffette!" we begged.

Sidelong glance, ears flattened, back raised, she sprang into the air, landed on all four paws.

"How lovely! Dance!"

Mouffette leaped higher still, took another bound, threatening us with that terrible profile.

"Dance, Mouffette!"

She jumped, came down on all four paws, rose again, cast us a wicked look.

She was prepared to dance all night now that she'd found the game of scaring us to death.

Dance the brief flames of the candles in their glasses! Dance the amused glimmer in the eyes of the humans all around! And dance in the middle of our circle the little black-and-white form dizzy with its success!

The Mass
of the Swallows

Adjacent to the cow-pasture, behind a clipped cedar hedge and near the pond, stands a chapel with room for about fifteen people. A rustic cottage close by that I call "the little presbytery" is used as retreat house by My Uncle the Curé, Aimé's brother, when he comes home to rest. On these occasions he celebrates Mass in the chapel. To announce Mass he pulls a cord that rings a bell with a very thin sound. On days of high wind it can just be heard. At once people set out from all corners of the plateau: several of Lucienne's children; little Claude in his best suit and a cap; Berthe without fail; some of Monsieur Simon's family; strangers if there are any; I myself from time to time.

I went by way of the pasture that day. Roused by the tiny sound that recalled the tinkling of the bell worn one summer by the late lamented Rover, the cows trailed after me to the fence and tried to gain admittance on my heels into the sacred enclosure. Did they believe that the light tinkling would lead them to some vestige of the deceased, who has left such pleasant memories behind? Or were they simply consumed with curiosity to learn at last why so many of their acquaintances gathered like this in broad daylight, seemingly to do nothing? Whatever their reason, they remained at the fence all through Mass, standing devoutly.

As My Uncle the Curé always leaves the door of the chapel open—otherwise we'd stifle—the cows in their places could follow the Mass quite well out of the corner of their eyes.

My Uncle the Curé, who might have been seen an instant before relaxing in his old corduroy trousers and turtleneck sweater, now appeared in a chasuble embroidered with gold thread. Little Claude's eyes almost popped out of his head in wonder. My Uncle the Curé greeted us with a few friendly words, we being his neighbours, then absorbed himself in the Mass.

We all had our noses more or less touching the altar. Standing so close to one another, we should have felt cramped. Yet it was quite otherwise because of the open door, which admitted the pool with its limpid surface, the endless blue folds of the hills, and a bit of river and sky near the point of Ile aux Coudres. Sometimes a freighter drifted into our field of vision, enveloped in its smoke. Thus into this insignificant little chapel the distance penetrated.

When Mass had begun, the swallows arrived in a tremendous flurry as if to make us overlook their tardiness. They skimmed the surface of the pond with their breasts, sprinkling us from afar as if with holy water.

"Nobis-nobis," we heard them say with their little mouse cries.

They apparently were not aware that the Mass is no longer said in Latin.

"Oh Christ, have mercy," said My Uncle the Curé.

"Nobis-nobis," replied the tiny voices of the swallows.

"Have mercy," intoned little Claude in his clear singing voice.

"Mercy," breathed the cows at the fence in a great sigh.

They pushed against one another, but not roughly, trying to get a better view of the inside of the chapel. Then up trotted Miquette, little Claude's German shepherd. With a severe look the boy riveted the dog to the door-sill. She lay there, her body outside, only her muzzle in the church. And, eyes raised to us and to the officiant, paws together, she had an air of such piety that only the most stony-hearted could have sent her away.

"The Lord be with you," said the priest.

"And also with you."

The atmosphere, which had been charged with electricity all day, crackled. Thunder sounded in the distance. The hills rolled with its growling. And suddenly the storm was upon us. You would have thought the rain was doing its best to drive nails through the flimsy roof that protected us. It jostled the bell in its tiny belfry. The entire chapel seemed about to be carried off by the wind. The hills were drowned. Of the vast expanse of river and sky of a moment ago nothing remained but a vague sallow tint. The swallows had found shelter. With cautious movements of her folded paws, Miquette wriggled forward till she was entirely under cover, except for her tail, which she had not the audacity to draw into the church.

The cows by the fence could scarcely be distinguished in the deluge though they did not stir. For a moment I thought I could glimpse Prince behind them, trying with his great mournful eyes to see into the chapel. Then he withdrew. Or the mist absorbed him.

"On the night he was betrayed," said the priest, "he

took bread and gave you thanks and praise. He broke the bread, gave it to his disciples and said: 'Take this, all of you, and eat it: this is my body which will be given up for you.'"

We had forgotten that he was My Uncle the Curé. Now he was only the priest. Just as we for this instant at least were only children of the Father.

As abruptly as it had broken, the storm subsided. A luminous hole appeared, as if a small window were being opened in the high wall of the sky.

The swallows took to the air again and, as they passed the doorway, we heard their almost imperceptible response, "Nobis-nobis."

"When supper was ended, he took the cup. Again he gave you thanks and praise, gave the cup to his disciples and said: 'Take this, all of you, and drink from it.'"

The marvellous story unfolded once again and once again held us enthralled.

At a single look from little Claude, Miquette slithered out of the chapel. Now she was only half inside, her head almost dry, her back damp, her tail so saturated you could have wrung a stoupful from it.

Little Claude was first to go forward to receive the host in his hand, which he extended as if expecting a treasure. His face shone like the freshly washed countryside around. Miquette gave him a look we had never seen before, humble and proud at once, as if she had a king for master.

The young took communion in the new way, the rest of us in the old.

Suddenly, rubbing their wings together, the crickets decided to play an accompaniment to the communion. The cows by the fence almost dislocated their necks in their efforts to see what we were eating. Prince reappeared for a moment, head towering over the cows, then he vanished again. Mass has never held much charm for him, dull-witted as he is.

86

"May almighty God bless you," said the priest.

"Nobis-nobis," entreated the tiny voices of the swallows, for once putting their response just right.

The priest opened wide his arms.

"Go in the peace of Christ."

On the doorstep we were dazzled by the brightness of the landscape. All its dust had been carried away by the downpour. Each leaf now held a bubble of water. The sky was a gleaming matter. One by one the hills were reborn to our sight with the contours we have always known and yet seeming to be revealed to us afresh. Then a rainbow appeared, stretching from one side of the pond to the other like a suspended bridge. Part of it crumbled away and now, like the bridge at Avignon, it stopped in mid-span.

"Nobis-nobis," the scatterbrained swallows resumed. Having served Mass all askew, they seemed not to know that it was over.

Then Berthe's grey cat came hurrying along the path through the high grass, bitterly disappointed at having missed Mass, which she dearly loves to attend, seated on her tail.

Miquette rubbed against little Claude and looked up at him with profound respect. The boy stroked her forehead gently. The cows scattered quickly to let us pass, still staring at us fixedly.

It was as if our domestic animals felt for us today something very close to adoration.

Or perhaps a humble and confused jealousy.

"What do they know that we don't know? What have they seen today? Received? That touches their faces for a moment with such beauty?"

The Day
Martine Went Down
to the River

I

Tontine is getting on in years. When we gather in the evening in Aimé's kitchen, she dozes. She has no interest in our talk of the cost of living, inflation and the Vietnam War. Her slumber is broken by nightmares that must be violent for occasionally she whines and we see her tremble all over. For a long time now she hasn't danced with joy when she hears us mention the river. Out of consideration for her aged bones we avoid pronouncing the word in her presence. We use evasions. We say, for instance, "Shall we go down ... to ... to the edge of the water?" We have finally stricken even this word from our vocabulary for she has come to associate it with the river, or rather with the sea, as we usually call the St. Lawrence in these parts.

Sometimes as we fumble around the subject, she opens her eyes and gives us a look marked with the distrust that comes to very old people when a sort of protective conspiracy is woven around them. And the aggrieved expression in the eyes of the little dog reproaches us for no longer speaking openly in front of her.

But still very shrewd, she has caught onto the fact that when Berthe puts on her rubber boots, it's almost always to go down to the river. And the other evening when Berthe opened the boot and broom cupboard beneath the angle of the stairway, Tontine bounded to her feet. She tried, in the middle of the kitchen, to give one of those lively performances of former times, all laughing, frisking and supplications. Blind in one eye, her haunches and neck stiff, she succeeded in showing something of the joy that used to fill her in the days of her youth. For just as it is with human beings, the chief happiness of Tontine's old age comes from the memory that she was once young and full of life.

She makes me think of old cousin Martine when she came home after fifty years' exile in a lodging without air or vista to see the river once again before she died.

II

Her children brought her by car. It took four of them to help her out and half-carry her up the front steps and over to the nearest chair.

For a few days she sat rocking in the kitchen right beside the window that overlooks the sea, gazing at it with each forward movement of the chair.

"It's coming in," she kept saying. "It's still coming in. ..." Then, "It's beginning to go out. ... It's going out. ..."

At first this was all she could find to say about what had been perhaps the deepest attachment of her life, "It's coming in. ... It's going out. ..."

She had been given a room with a view of the river so that just before she slept and as soon as she wakened she had time to look at it again. Finally this was no longer sufficient.

One day we heard the mild little woman lamenting, "Isn't it a shame! Isn't it a pity! To come from so far away and not even go down to the river."

"Ho ho ho!" her eldest son Edgar replied with some severity. "Go down to the river! Put that idea right out of your head, Mother. You have to hang onto a chair even to get around the house. And yet you want to go down that big hill. Do try to be sensible, Mother."

"I'm much stronger now," said Martine defensively.

This was true; she could now manage on her own the seven or eight steps from her bed to the window to have one last look before she slept at the sea as it rose or fell.

Her other son, Déodat, though less impatient, also tried to reason with her.

"It's pretty nice anyway, isn't it, Mother, that we've brought you to spend two good weeks at home? Remember all the trouble we had getting you down those steep steps from the third floor. You musn't demand too much."

And so, having set their mother to rights, they went off to spend the day fishing for trout in the mountain brook.

Martine was silent for a few minutes, staring into the distance, then, unaware that she was speaking out loud, began again, "If just once before I die, I could go down to the river!"

"The river! The river! You can see it from here, Mother!"

Startled out of her reverie, Martine looked with astonishment at whoever it was who was speaking with such lack of comprehension; she sighed, then gave up trying to give an explanation. There are so many things the old give up trying to explain to the young, which the young will not understand till the day when they in turn give up trying to explain them to others younger still. And so the muffled circle of the generations closes.

But Berthe, though far from old herself, understood the keen desire that was tormenting the small arthritic body of Cousin Martine.

"Build up your strength a little more, Cousin," she said one day. "Then you and I will go down to the sea together."

"You'd do that! You'd bother with me?"

Deep in the wrinkled face, her eyes shone so brightly that we glimpsed a little of the young Martine we had never known.

I joined in. "I'll come too. It will be better with three."

"My children! How sweet you are! What a lovely day we'll have!"

"We'll help you over the roughest spots," said Berthe. "We'll even carry you a bit."

"As far as that goes," Aimé suggested, full of good will, "why couldn't I take you down in the tractor?"

Martine gave him an indignant look.

"In a tractor to the river!"

She burst into fresh clear laughter.

"In a tractor to the river! At my age! Just think of that! In a tractor!"

And it was as if she were saying, "To church in a tractor!"

Aimé, a little disconcerted, said defensively, "I was just trying to be helpful . . . really."

In fact, there were four of us to go down to the river. For Tontine was of the party. At the sudden confusion in the house, she had suspected that an event of some importance was afoot. When just as we were about to leave, Martine in a black satinette dress asked for her city hat as well, Tontine was overcome with excitement and cried heartbreakingly, "I want to go! I want to go too!"

"She may as well come," said Berthe finally. "At the speed we'll be travelling, it won't be any harder on her than wearing herself out trying to get through the screen door. Come along then, my little idiot."

Enlivened by the keen air of the summer morning

and the intoxication of the departure, Martine went a good bit of the way alone. Her movements were trembling and uncertain but her face was as exalted as that of a child taking its first steps.

When we reached the fence, we grasped the tiny old woman under the arms, hoisted her over the wire and deposited her on the other side. Martine was still laughing when we joined her, we two also over the wire and Tontine beneath.

Then as she was a little tired, as much from laughing as from walking, Berthe and I made a sort of chair out of our crossed hands and here Martine took her place, steadying herself with an arm around our shoulders. When I used to play as a child at crossing the jungle, I was sometimes the potentate who permitted herself to be carried in this manner but usually one of the slave porters of the potentate. Martine was choking with laughter at finding herself borne aloft above the uncut hay. From time to time she gave one of us a light tap of encouragement on the shoulder. Tontine brought up the rear, lips drawn back as if she too were laughing—or perhaps simply amazed. For never before in our region had she witnessed the spectacle of a person being carried on a chair made of hands through the high grass. She was not jealous, however, and when Martine let one of her hands trail, she licked it gently.

At the edge of the birch and alder thicket where the hill begins, we halted and seated Cousin Martine on a smooth rock. Though she was incredibly tiny, weighing scarcely more than eighty pounds, we were breathless. So we sat down beside her.

"Poor children," she said, out of breath herself. "I'm almost killing you."

We said no, not in the least, we were ready to go on, and we began to suck at tender grass, which we gathered around us.

It was a dim leafy spot with no view of the river.

Conversation became melancholy. We discovered that Cousin Martine was not very different from the birds of the shore, almost light-hearted one moment, sad the next.

"In Hochelaga," she said, "I wasn't really so far from the river. I could have walked down there more often. But the few times I did, I scarcely recognized it. Along the shore you couldn't even see the water. Just banana peel, orange rinds and dirty papers thrown from boats. And you could breathe nothing but oil. Just once I closed my eyes and caught, coming from far away, the faint, faint scent of the tide. Then I lost it."

She fell silent, hands folded across her hollow stomach.

It was difficult to accept the idea that from this thin small body had come great heavy Edgar, weighing in at almost two hundred pounds, and Maurice who was nearly six feet tall. Even the daughters looked like big solidly planted trees beside their reedlike little mother.

"I had fourteen altogether," Martine told us, "fourteen children. Nowadays women with two or three to raise complain, 'It's too expensive. It's too much work.' I had fourteen to raise," she repeated proudly.

Then sadness overcame the joy in the cracked voice.

"I lost more than are left to me. There was Geraldine ... so tiny and finely made, my Geraldine. After her, Marie-Ange, perhaps my prettiest one."

A herring gull lamented in the distance as he passed again and again across the patch of sky we could see from our shelter beneath the trees.

In just as doleful a voice Martine told of her dead children.

"Horace who was so sweet. ... Never saw such a sweet little child. Then my Solange. ..."

Tontine, who still possessed her wonderful gift for sensing the grief of human beings, approached Martine and looked deeply and with compassion into her eyes.

And the little old human mother looked back just as deeply at the little old animal and stroked Tontine's forehead with a sympathetic hand.

Then we hoisted Martine onto the seat made of our crossed hands and off we went again.

"Come, Cousin," said Berthe. "This is no day for sorrow. The river's awaiting you. You mustn't show it a sad face."

"That's very true," said Martine, beginning to smile again under the brim of her hat.

Suddenly she decided, "What use is this?" She took off the hat and hung it on the branch of a tree where it could easily be retrieved on the way back.

The wind stirring her thin hair, she laughed again with her light mocking laughter.

"What an idea of Aimé's to take me down by tractor!"

She turned to measure with approval the distance we'd already covered. "It's much better to go on foot like us three."

"Yes, indeed," we agreed, "it's very much better to go on foot like us three."

A little later, unable to walk another step, we set Martine down on the slope of the wooded path.

"Poor children," she said, though perhaps without quite as much compassion as before. "I'm tiring you. It's hard going, eh? But at your age one recovers quickly."

Curiously, Berthe and I, who just the evening before had been telling each other we were no longer good for anything much, felt brisk and energetic today beside Martine. Perhaps the most miraculous gift of the very old is that they make those who are not really young feel youthful again.

We picked Martine up, put her down, picked her up once more. At the end of the wooded path where the river appears in all its immensity, we set her down finally for, suddenly imperious and independent, she wanted to approach it "on my own two feet."

However, she had to accept a little more help from us to cross the railway track, then a field, and to navigate a final rough passage between huge rocks.

And now we were right beside the river. With a sort of impatience she pushed us away with both hands at once and went on alone, over the pebbles, through the coarse sand. She did not waver. Her entire being carried her forward, a soul straining towards God.

Leaving her alone with the river, we withdrew a short distance, first warning her, "Watch out for the big waves after the passage of a ship."

She flung a look over her shoulder that informed us: "There's no need for such as you to tell me about *my* river."

Tontine also appeared anxious. She fussed around Martine for a moment, asking us with a worried look, "Isn't it dangerous to leave her all by herself?" Then she went to sit in the place that had been hers for years, well sheltered behind the boulders.

Martine stood motionless. At her feet waves broke with a tender whisper. Around the small figure in the black skirt all was blue today: the water right into the farthest distance, the tiered line of hills over towards Les Eboulements, the faint shadow of Ile aux Coudres barely visible above the water.

She stood there on the threshold of immensity, with her regret for her dead children and the recollection of the troubles she had endured, with her bereavements and her sorrows, with the memory of her endless waiting for this return to the river. And it was all being weighed in a mysterious balance: the cruel waiting and this radiant instant today. And who can say that the instant did not tip the scales?

The teasing wind blew up the old-fashioned skirt that hung long on her calves and dishevelled her hair. Patiently as she had lived, she smoothed down her skirt, then her hair, tucking in the loose strands. Then she turned to us a face on which lost youth shone for a moment like the reflection of a distant sun.

"I almost think I'll take off my shoes. Put my feet in the water. Seems to me it might do me good."

We went down to help her. She had seated herself on one of the stones. We removed the heavy shoes that had been resoled and mended several times.

"They're the only ones in which I'm reasonably comfortable," she said in excuse.

We drew off the thick black stockings. Her feet appeared, as small and white as a child's but incredibly twisted. And it was on these poor insignificant feet that Martine had got through her hard life. She looked at them as if surprised herself at all they'd been able to bear.

"They've held me up at times long enough to iron twenty-five men's shirts at a stretch."

We rubbed them gently, then accompanied her to the edge of the water. She went in valiantly, hitching up her skirt. Tontine had come down too and asked us with a troubled look, "Do you really think you should let her do it?" And she sat down to keep a close watch on this old cousin who was behaving so oddly.

Daringly Martine advanced a step farther. The water encircled her pale ankles. The sea breeze bathed her worn face.

In the vast unfurlment of water and sky she made a stain scarcely larger than the black bird beating its wings on the shore. Did one of the oldest crows think it had found its counterpart? It circled several times above Cousin Martine, then gave a sort of cry of surprise, "Can it be little Martine come back? The little girl who loved nothing as much as paddling in the water?"

"Not possible, not possible," croaked another ancient crow which was also renowned for its memory of former times. "Today little Martine would be seventy-eight ... seventy-nine years old. It couldn't be little Martine."

"It is so little Martine. See. She's still paddling in the water."

Martine followed the conversation with a wondering expression as if she grasped something of what was being said in the sky.

For my part, the more I looked at her the more I was reminded of those pilgrims of the Ganges in Benares, whom one sees with loincloths tucked up, frighteningly thin but their faces illuminated with fervour.

We finally removed our own shoes and joined her. I think she was pleased to have us at her side in case she stumbled. But she didn't want anyone to take her hand or, for the moment, speak to her. She had suddenly become aware of the invisible as if behind this day that she had waited for all her life, she glimpsed another more radiant still. And she needed to be alone and all attention to recognize intimations of the unknown.

Suddenly, barefoot on the rim of the summer sky, she began to ask questions—doubtless the only ones that matter.

"Why do we live? What are we sent to do on this earth? Why do we suffer so and feel lonely? What are we waiting for? What is at the end of it all? Eh? Eh?"

Her tone was not sorrowful. Troubled perhaps at the beginning. But gradually it became confident. As if, though she didn't quite know the answer, she already sensed that it was good. And she was content at last that she had lived.

Then almost at once she drooped with weariness, with emotion and from touching the mysterious goal.

It was for them both the last journey down to the river.

Tontine was found dead one morning in her place behind the stove.

As for Martine, scarcely had she returned to the cramped little flat with no outlook and no light than she departed for those open spaces she had longed for all her life.

The Day's Visitors

Today a number of my friends dropped by to pay me a visit.

Some came that I didn't even see but merely heard.

Among others the catbird.

My transistor radio beside me, I was in my swing, listening to a Bach cantata broadcast from Sainte-Anne-de-la-Pocatière.

Wonder of wonders! In some capital of the world, musicians interpreted the cantata, a tape fixed the music and now it was being transmitted across the river by La Pocatière to blend with the choir of my pines as they sang in full voice, "Hallelujah! The day is magnificent!"

Then the catbird joined in. He played a sort of accompaniment on the beak-flute. A tiny air of great delicacy, scarcely standing out above the instrumental ensemble.

The music from Sainte-Anne-de-la-Pocatière concluded and the flautist, carried by his own momentum, went on alone for a moment and stopped in the middle of a trill, abashed at having drawn attention to himself.

Then from a clump of cedars came a bird so modest looking in his slate-grey garb that I would never have taken him for the brilliant soloist of a minute ago. I had barely caught a glimpse of him when he left for a concert tour among my neighbours. And their gain was my loss.

Next seven cedar waxwings arranged themselves on various levels of the same tree, as if to be seen in all their beauty from every side at once.

Thereupon some of my human friends arrived. They saw the splendid birds in the tree and, as they are city folk and not spoiled by such sights, they exclaimed, "Ah! What magnificent creatures!"

Now that they had produced their effect, the cedar waxwings could depart. Which they did without further ado.

For a few minutes there were no more bird arrivals. My human guests were talking too loudly.

Except for the familiar crows that call to me every day as they pass, "How do you do?"

Ever since they surprised me one day, seated in my swing with a notebook on my knees, writing stories, they've been very careful not to disturb me. But even so, they can't bring themselves to pass over my house without at least saying, "Good day. Work well."

Later some herring gulls came to fly above our tedious earthly life. Sometimes in the course of the summer, no one quite knows why, they leave the river and their usual existence to venture quite far inland. On these occasions they soar over fields, hedges and houses. Do they feel a sudden urge to exchange lives with the land birds? Is it this or something else? We hear their cry, so similar to a squeaking gate, from close at hand. Yet the curious sound is beautiful to hear and so mysterious no one has ever learned to grasp its meaning.

But the herring gull is admirable above all for its flight.

We watched them glide, bank steeply on the edge of

one wing, lean back, you might think, into the wind and then right themselves—all their subtleties.

Their performance completed, the gulls too left the stage.

Next came a flock of swallows, also to be admired for their flight, all darts and spurts.

"Ah, swallows!" cried my friends.

It is a fact, this bird need only appear to be applauded. Never, to my knowledge, is any other bird made so much fuss over. True, the others in their modesty don't care in the least. So for about ten minutes nothing existed but the swallows.

Then a quarter of an hour later, as we were chatting loudly in the garden, into our conversation burst a bit of a phrase of neither rhyme nor reason, "Hast thou seen Fred-er-ic, Fred-er-ic, Fred-er-ic?"

It was the white-throated sparrow.

He sings when he pleases—whether there are guests with me or not, whether the day is fair or cloudy. He has his hour to sing and sing he will.

He has his hiding place too but you mustn't tell; it's just below the third branch from the bottom of the huge dark-green spruce next to my twisted birch.

My friends had begun to discuss the latest novels and current literary trends and the little fool kept on trilling "Hast thou seen ..."

"What is that tiresome refrain?" asked Edmonde de Saint-Martin, the friend who talked the most.

I told her it was one of my very punctual and friendly visitors and added that each of us, either by the tone of voice or the nose or one of our other characteristics, is akin to some bird.

"Just listen to her!" said Edmonde de Saint-Martin mockingly and in a tone so reminiscent of "Hast thou seen ..." that we all smiled—except Edmonde de Saint-Martin, who hadn't caught the resemblance.

Next there was a general rushing about. Someone—

Alice? Adrienne?—had caught sight of a hummingbird.

"It's here."

"No, it's there."

We were like mad things, running this way and that, trying to distinguish the hummingbird among the flowers.

"Do you see him?"

"No, do you?"

Finally we all spied the tiny helicopter at the same instant, rising and falling as it fed on flower after flower.

We saw its long beak burrow into the calix of a lily, withdraw, then prick the heart of a bluebell.

But the body of the bird we could scarcely glimpse, it's so small and swift, so similar in colour to the flowers it haunts.

Moving from one to the other, it appears to give each a peck and to love them all but only in passing.

"What a marvel!" cried Alice.

I put an arm around her neck. With us Alice is in a sense our hummingbird.

"Ah," she says to one of us, "there's no one quite like you," then turns and says to another, "Precious, you have no equal," and to still another, "Angel of my heart, you're absolutely unique."

And even though we know Alice repeats herself, we would rather have her refrain than that of the long-faced-who-dole-out-their-tidbits.

"Dear hummingbird," I said.

And the astonishing thing is that she didn't seem any too delighted with the compliment.

Soon afterwards my friends said they must leave if they were to be home before dark. We embraced in the house. Then on the steps. Then at the gate. (It is a fact that in the country people embrace more often than in the city.) Then they all waved as the car drew away. I was alone.

At this hour, which is always a little sad, when friends have just left and evening is about to fall, the world seems empty. I find myself circling aimlessly, not quite knowing what to do with myself, something is missing. I feel alone and finally I go and sit in the swing.

Then the robin appears. The robin is a bird with no great talent for flight or song, some say, though I myself enjoy his cheerful whistling like that of a man walking along with his hands in his pockets.

He is clad in perfectly plain grey-brown, his one adornment his pleasant close-fitting rusty-coloured vest. He arrives on foot. By day he can be seen perching on a branch or, on occasion, on one of the telephone wires. But in the evening he is just a little pedestrian like you and me. And his roundabout begins. I take four dancing steps. At the fifth, stop, thrust out my chest. Spy you out of the corner of my eye. And go back to the beginning: four dancing steps, chest out, quick sidelong glance.

Thus for hours, never losing patience, the robin keeps me company, inscribing a hundred times, a thousand, his wide circle around the swing.

I could probably get him to eat out of my hand, as the saying goes. But to what purpose? He comes as soon as I am alone, as soon as there is no more sound in me or around me. He was nowhere an instant ago. Now he never leaves me.

And I take my four dancing steps. And I thrust out my chest. And I glance at you out of the corner of my eye. And find that you look a bit sad this evening. Yet you needn't feel badly. It's true, there's always a painful moment when the day is about to end. I know something about that. One has more need than ever of a friend.

We sat up late that night, the robin and I. When it was almost dark, he was still there making his trip around the swing, after every fourth step giving me a lightning glance.

In the dark blue of the twilight I could just discern my companion, who was perhaps waiting for me to move before he retired.

So I played a trick on him. I gathered up my things and went into the house, acting as if I were going in for good. I closed the door, put on the lights. I let a moment pass.

Then I went back out very quietly and returned to the swing. There was no one there. The robin was perhaps already asleep, head tucked under his wing. But I no longer felt lonely. I was waiting for the first shooting stars.

The Night
of the Fireflies

Night had come. By now my friend the robin must be fast asleep in the hollow I know, in the thickest part of the hedge. God watch over his little ephemeral life! Shooting stars plummeted through the sky. I made a wish. I wished that the children of these regions would never tire of listening to their planet Earth. Even though in our day we receive news from the moon.

The stars shone brilliantly, then paled. Now they were half effaced, like tarnished nails in the ceiling of a chapel long abandoned to its memories. And I knew suddenly why the stars had dimmed. It was to give the fireflies their turn to shine. For now they appeared in their hundreds in the mild and tranquil night.

There was still a trace of music clinging to the tops of the trees. You might have thought they were quivering in their dreams. I could not resign myself to going in. On some rare nights one feels that it would be a crime not to wait up with them a little longer. Not this time because of the weight of the world's anguish but because the darkness was permeated with the most mysterious joy. And now came the bearers of the flame.

On the freshly mown grass they shone in brief bursts, like the intermittent beam of the lighthouse that signals to ships the passage round the tip of Ile aux Coudres.

On the dark grass innumerable tiny lighthouses flickered on and off as if to guide invisible travellers of the night. It might be you, it might be me, who often have to seek our way.

Then the little creatures rose into the air and now they were ballet dancers. And spin. And turn on the spot. And pivot, a diadem on the forehead. The sky was full of them. It was impossible to follow all of them at once. Who invented this choreography of such tireless fantasy? Fire above, fire a little farther away, and fire suddenly almost in my hand. Had I been quicker I might have grasped the flying flame. Berthe has told me that as a child she caught more than one firefly. I myself would fear that I might shatter the delicate mechanism that releases the swift blue flame. And I am troubled by the thought that by day I might mistake for a common insect one of these celebrants of fire.

Why do they exist? It is said that they announce hot weather but no doubt they announce very much more.

And now they were a little calmer. No longer dancing in the air, they had become ordinary strollers. They moved back and forth midway between earth and sky, the fire of their little lamps revealed or hidden according to the twists and turns of the mysterious promenade.

The night was indescribably tender. One might have believed oneself on the threshold of the infinite, ready to touch at last the goal to which, unknown to ourselves, our spirits strain. The brief flames continued to flutter through the blurred dark of the night.

Their existence is fugitive. Perhaps fireflies live only long enough to give forth their fleeting light.

Like all of us.

Fortunate are those who at least once before they are extinguished shine with their full light.

Caught in God's fire.

The Dead Child

Why then did the memory of that dead child seek me out in the very midst of the summer that sang?

When till then no intimation of sorrow had come to me through the dazzling revelations of that season.

I had just arrived in a very small village in Manitoba to finish the school year as replacement for a teacher who had fallen ill or simply, for all I know, become discouraged.

The principal of the Normal School had called me to his office towards the end of my year's study. "Well," he said, "there's a school available for the month of June. It's not much but it's an opportunity. When the time comes for you to apply for a permanent position, you'll be able to say you've had experience. Believe me, it's a help."

And so I found myself at the beginning of June in that very poor village—just a few shacks built on sand, with nothing around it but spindly spruce trees. "A month," I asked myself, "will that be long enough for me to become attached to the children or for the children to

111

become attached to me? Will a month be worth the effort?"

Perhaps the same calculation was in the minds of the children who presented themselves at school that first day of June—"Is this teacher going to stay long enough to be worth the effort?"—for I had never seen children's faces so dejected, so apathetic, or perhaps sorrowful. I had had so little experience. I myself was hardly more than a child.

Nine o'clock came. The room was hot as an oven. Sometimes in Manitoba, especially in the sandy areas, an incredible heat settles in during the first days of June.

Scarcely knowing where or how to begin, I opened the attendance book and called the roll. The names were for the most part very French and today they still return to my memory, like this, for no reason: Madeleine Bérubé, Josephat Brisset, Emilien Dumont, Cécile Lépine. . . .

But most of the children who rose and answered "Present, mamzelle," when their names were called had the slightly narrowed eyes, warm colouring and jet black hair that told of métis blood.

They were beautiful and exquisitely polite; there was really nothing to reproach them for except the inconceivable distance they maintained between themselves and me. It crushed me. "Is this what children are like then," I asked myself with anguish, "untouchable, barricaded in some region where you can't reach them?"

I came to the name Yolande Chartrand.

No one answered. It was becoming hotter by the minute. I wiped a bit of perspiration from my forehead. I repeated the name and, when there was still no answer, I looked up at faces that seemed to me completely indifferent.

Then from the back of the classroom, above the buzzing of flies, there arose a voice I at first couldn't place. "She's dead, mamzelle. She died last night."

Perhaps even more distressing than the news was the calm level tone of the child's voice. As I must have seemed unconvinced, all the children nodded gravely as if to say, "It's true."

Suddenly a sense of impotence greater than any I can remember weighed upon me.

"Ah," I said, lost for words.

"She's already laid out," said a boy with eyes like coals. "They're going to bury her for good tomorrow."

"Ah," I repeated.

The children seemed a little more relaxed now and willing to talk, in snatches and at long intervals.

A boy in the middle of the room offered, "She got worse the last two months."

We looked at one another in silence for a long time, the children and I. I now understood that the expression in their eyes that I had taken for indifference was a heavy sadness. Much like this stupefying heat. And we were only at the beginning of the day.

"Since Yolande ... has been laid out," I suggested, "and she was your schoolmate ... and would have been my pupil ... would you like ... after school at four o'clock ... for us to go and visit her?"

On the small, much too serious faces there appeared the trace of a smile, wary, still very sad but a sort of smile just the same.

"It's agreed then, we'll go to visit her, her whole class."

From that moment, despite the enervating heat and the sense that haunted us all, I feel sure, that human efforts are all ultimately destined to a sort of failure, the children fixed their attention as much as possible on what I was teaching and I did my best to rouse their interest.

At five past four I found most of them waiting for me at the door, a good twenty children but making no more noise than if they were being kept in after school. Several of them went ahead to show me the way. Others pressed around me so closely I could scarcely move. Five or six of the smaller ones took me by the hand or the shoulder and pulled me forward gently as if they were leading a blind person. They did not talk, merely held me enclosed in their circle.

Together, in this way, we followed a track through the sand. Here and there thin spruce trees formed little clumps. The air was now barely moving. In no time the village was behind us—forgotten, as it were.

We came to a wooden cabin standing in isolation among the little trees. Its door was wide open, so we were able to see the dead child from quite far off. She had been laid out on rough boards suspended between two straight chairs set back to back. There was nothing else in the room. Its usual contents must have been crowded into the only other room of the house for, besides a stove and table and a few pots on the floor, I could see a bed and a mattress piled with clothes. But no chairs. Clearly the two used as supports for the boards on which the dead child lay were the only ones in the house.

The parents had undoubtedly done all they could for their child. They had covered her with a clean sheet. They had given her a room to herself. Her mother, probably, had arranged her hair in the two very tight braids that framed the thin face. But some pressing need had sent them away: perhaps the purchase of a coffin in town or a few more boards to make her one themselves. At any rate, the dead child was alone in the room that had been emptied for her—alone, that is to say, with the flies. A faint odour of death must have attracted them. I saw one with a blue body walk over her forehead. I immediately placed myself near her head and began to move my hand back and forth to drive the flies away.

The child had a delicate little face, very wasted, with the serious expression I had seen on the faces of most of the children here, as if the cares of the adults had crushed

114

them all too early. She might have been ten or eleven years old. If she had lived a little longer, I reminded myself, she would have been one of my pupils. She would have learned something from me. I would have given her something to keep. A bond would have been formed between me and this little stranger—who knows, perhaps even for life.

As I contemplated the dead child, those words "for life"—as if they implied a long existence—seemed to me the most rash and foolish of all the expressions we use so lightly.

In death the child looked as if she were regretting some poor little joy she had never known. I continued at least to prevent the flies from settling upon her. The children were watching me. I realized that they now expected everything from me, though I didn't know much more than they and was just as confused. Still I had a sort of inspiration.

"Don't you think Yolande would like to have someone with her always till the time comes to commit her to the ground?"

The faces of the children told me I had struck the right note.

"We'll take turns then, four or five around her every two hours, until the funeral."

They agreed with a glow in their dark eyes.

"We must be careful not to let the flies touch Yolande's face."

They nodded to show they were in agreement. Standing around me, they now felt a trust in me so complete it terrified me.

In a clearing among the spruce trees a short distance away, I noticed a bright pink stain on the ground whose source I didn't yet know. The sun slanted upon it, making it flame, the one moment in this day that had been touched by a certain grace.

"What sort of girl was she?" I asked.

At first the children didn't understand. Then a boy of about the same age said with tender seriousness, "She was smart, Yolande."

The other children looked as if they agreed.

"And did she do well in school?"

"She didn't come very often this year. She was always being absent."

"Our teacher before last this year said Yolande could have done well."

"How many teachers have you had this year?"

"You're the third, mamzelle. I guess the teachers find it too lonesome here."

"What did Yolande die of?"

"T.B., mamzelle," they replied with a single voice, as if this was the customary way for children to die around here.

They were eager to talk about her now. I had succeeded in opening the poor little doors deep within them that no one perhaps had ever much wanted to see opened. They told me moving facts about her brief life. One day on her way home from school—it was in February; no, said another, in March—she had lost her reader and wept inconsolably for weeks. To study her lesson after that, she had to borrow a book from one of the others—and I saw on the faces of some of them that they'd grudged lending their readers and would always regret this. Not having a dress for her first communion, she entreated till her mother finally made her one from the only curtain in the house: "the one from this room ... a beautiful lace curtain, mamzelle."

"And did Yolande look pretty in her lace curtain dress?" I asked.

They all nodded deeply, in their eyes the memory of a pleasant image.

I studied the silent little face. A child who had loved books, solemnity and decorous attire. Then I glanced again at that astonishing splash of pink in the melancholy landscape. I realized suddenly that it was a mass of wild roses. In June they open in great sheets all over Manitoba, growing from the poorest soil. I felt some alleviation.

"Let's go and pick some roses for Yolande."

On the children's faces there appeared the same slow smile of gentle sadness I had seen when I suggested visiting the body.

In no time we were gathering roses. The children were not yet cheerful, far from that, but I could hear them at least talking to one another. A sort of rivalry had gripped them. Each vied to see who could pick the most roses or the brightest, those of a deep shade that was almost red.

From time to time one tugged at my sleeve, "Mamzelle, see the lovely one I've found!"

On our return we pulled them gently apart and scattered petals over the dead child. Soon only her face emerged from the pink drift. Then—how could this be? —it looked a little less forlorn.

The children formed a ring around their schoolmate and said of her without the bitter sadness of the morning, "She must have got to heaven by this time."

Or, "She must be happy now."

I listened to them, already consoling themselves as best they could for being alive.

But why, oh why, did the memory of that dead child seek me out today in the very midst of the summer that sang?

Was it brought to me just now by the wind with the scent of roses?

A scent I have not much liked since the long ago June when I went to that poorest of villages—to acquire, as they say, experience.

The Islands

It is not in clear weather that one can best decipher the distance. Under storm clouds or just before the onset of the bitter cold, we in our part of the world can see some little islands in the open river that are never visible at other times. But when we've had them as companions for only a day or so, they drift away into a sort of dream existence where from time to time we can grasp the vague outline of first one and then another for an instant more.

In the torpid heat of summer the islands vanish completely. For weeks at a time we don't see them even once far across the river near Montmagny. In fact, there is no more open river. On those warm singing days of almost no horizon, we live confined and rocked by the west wind, held in cocoons of faintly whispering water and rustling leaves. And unhappiness seems far away. We find ourselves almost forgetting to think about the islands.

It seems that there are twenty-one in all scattered between Ile d'Orléans and Ile aux Coudres and that only two or three are inhabited. As against those few that are alive with lighted windows at night, visiting back and forth, and the sound of human voices, the greater number are as silent as in the first days of creation. Only foghorns reach them in the splashing immensity of the river. During the summer some sailor on the deck of a freighter that has strayed a little way off course may see one or other of them barely rising above the water and have the impression that he has discovered "his" island.

But all that singing summer we of the north shore had not caught sight of the islands over by the south shore more than once or twice.

Came the sharp days of fall. In the houses animals and people drew closer to the fire. And it was then, strangely, that the south shore drew closer to us so that suddenly, with unusual clarity, we observed churches, roofs and even barns that only the day before we could not see at all. Closer too drew the islands near the south shore. One after the other they came in sight, born, you might say, when everything in nature was dying. Now they were all lined up against the dark blue horizon, twenty-one islands, some of them not much more than circles of land grass surrounded by sea grass.

We began to dream again.

"What are they like?" I asked Berthe for the hundredth time.

She replied that she knew very little about them though she could dimly remember hearing her father say that his own father used to row over to one or other of them in a chaloupe to cut wild hay.

"So they would sleep on one of the islands?"

"Yes, I daresay," said Berthe.

She thought she could recall tales of those days that had been passed down in the family for generations. The men had a tent, at the very least a piece of sail for shelter. Perhaps they used to make a hut out of branches. If there was a sudden storm as happens so frequently on the river at this time of year, they would have to wait two or three days, maybe even longer, for calm weather, huddled in their precarious refuge on one or other of those low tufts of grass. Meanwhile the women in their houses on the north shore would be half dead with anxiety.

The sky remained dark for several days and the uninhabited islands were with us for a while longer. They obsessed us.

"Berthe, I've never wanted to go anywhere as much as to one of those little islands."

She smiled patiently.

"It's not easy. We'd have to go to Quebec. Take the bus to the south shore. Go the long way round by land. At Montmagny find someone to take us to the islands by boat or helicopter. If we went by boat we'd have to have the tide with us."

"In short, to go that little way to those islands we'd need Joliet and Père Marquette."

"Or my grandfather," said Berthe.

While we'd been talking, jet planes had crossed the distant sky. We could not see them, just the trails of smoke that marked their passage. People to whom earth was as invisible as the jet was to us were on their way to London, Paris, Amsterdam.

Almost directly over our quiet little village jets begin their descent for Dorval. Altitude and atmospheric conditions permitting, we see their traces. Otherwise there is nothing to indicate that high above us are travellers returning from London, Paris, Amsterdam.

We grew tired of peering into the sky for signs of voyaging. They are so common now. Have lost their hold upon us. We returned to the islands over by Montmagny. They were all present for a moment more, strung out along the water like a series of points of suspension.

"Are there any animals on those islands?"

"If so, they must be very small. How could they have

crossed the water? Unless cats and dogs have been taken there to be abandoned. It would be a sad life for them. There must be plenty of birds, however."

All signs of voyaging had been obliterated from the high sky.

I began to dream again.

"Still we must at least go and discover our little islands, Berthe."

"Yes," she agreed. "We must."

The trouble was, we knew there was only one way: get up at daybreak, row across twenty miles of water, in some places dangerously rough, land in dark of night in a wild cove, make a fire, face what was faced by the people of bygone times.

We looked at one another ruefully. We are well aware that we are not of the stuff of which our ancestors were made. We tell ourselves in consolation that our courage lies elsewhere and I suppose this is true to some extent.

However, those insignificant little islands some sixteen or eighteen miles across the water continued to reproach us for a long time still.

Then the icy fogs enclosed us. The contours of the islands over by Montmagny disappeared. Like the birds that were leaving us for the winter.

What is the appeal of islands to our hearts?

Is it not that we are all lost children who long for a common shore?

Once More
to the Pool
of Monsieur Toong

That summer again Berthe and I walked along the railway track one evening to the pool of Monsieur Toong. Though the cordial greeting of the musician of the water would never again ring out, this was no reason to fail the solitary pine or the bluebells that draw from the rough ballast their colour so similar to the summer sky. Though all that delights us dies a little every day, we must not withdraw our hearts in advance.

And we were well recompensed. Once again the pool was inhabited. By whom? What a surprise it was to find Milord Mallard with his Lady. For there they were, revolving in silence in the ancient pool, which their presence made young again. There was still a hint of brightness at one side of the water and in this brighter patch the beautiful happy birds turned gravely around one another, wing brushing wing. And the water mirrored their gay costumes down to the smallest detail: the narrow forest-green hoods and yellow beaks, even the brilliant, slightly hard little eyes.

We did not try to engage them in conversation since

mallards seem little inclined for talk. Very preoccupied with themselves, they glanced at us rather loftily for a moment and went on circling one another politely.

We resumed our walk, as happy to find the pool alive once more as if we had seen a light suddenly turned on in a house that has long been dark. The beauty of the mallards did not replace the memory of Monsieur Toong. One joined the other.

Slightly farther on, another joyful surprise. All along this stretch of shore, on the banks of silt laid down through the years by tide and current, there are islets of the most pliant grass in the world, for twice a day at high tide the river covers it with vivifying water.

There is nothing abrupt here. Gently the water prevails upon the grasses, gently it withdraws; gently the wet grasses slow and calm the last undulations of the river.

But who was that flying around without fear or haste? Truly it was beyond belief; never before had I seen killdeers so tranquil and content with their lot.

Three of them—father, mother, child—were flying back and forth over the grassy verges whose green was darkening by the minute. They passed between this submerged green and the snowy white of the clouds in a sort of long circular promenade, seemingly with no desire to leave their enchanted circle. And for once I had encountered killdeers who were not contradicting one another. We could hear them quite clearly in the silence and peace of the twilight, talking together in low voices, and what they were saying seemed to be, "How peaceful it is here ... here ... here ..."

"Ah yes," we agreed, "how peaceful it is here ... here ... here. ... And do try not to forget it!"

But we were still full of unsatisfied curiosity.

"Why is it," we asked, "that other killdeers haven't also discovered these grassy verges, these thousands of blessed hiding places? Why didn't they find this refuge?

Why? Why?"

Then it seemed to us that a short distance away in the murmuring peace, the birds were reproaching us for our paltry human questions.

"All are not happy at the same moment," they reminded us. "One day it's one, the next day another ... some never, alas."

They soared out over the river, all three saying much the same thing in the same tone, a little weakened now by the distance so that we could believe we were hearing a single voice, "Here we are happy. ... Over there they are not. ... When everyone is happy together, it will be paradise ... paradise ... paradise. ..."

ABOUT THE AUTHOR

Gabrielle Roy's prominent role in the literature of Canada was established with the publication of her first novel in 1945. That book, *The Tin Flute* (or *Bonheur d'occasion,* as it was titled in the original French), was awarded the Prix Fémina, thus becoming the first Canadian work to win a major French literary prize. It also earned a Governor General's Award, plus medals from the Académie Française and the Académie Canadienne Française. In 1947, Miss Roy was elected to the Royal Society of Canada. She won a second Governor General's Award in 1957, this time for *Street of Riches,* which also won the Prix Duvernay. In 1971 the Quebec government awarded her the Prix David for her entire body of work.

Other books by Gabrielle Roy available in English are *Where Nests the Water Hen, The Cashier, The Hidden Mountain, The Road Past Altamont* and *Windflower.*